HILLOCK

ANNE SHERRY

authorHOUSE®

AuthorHouse™ UK
1663 Liberty Drive
Bloomington, IN 47403 USA
www.authorhouse.co.uk
Phone: 0800.197.4150

Published by AuthorHouse 08/14/2017

ISBN: 978-1-5462-8091-0 (sc)
ISBN: 978-1-5462-8090-3 (e)

CHAPTER ONE

Jemma Jackson, sat in her room. This was the third time this month she had been grounded.

Normally this wouldn't have bothered her, Jemma was an escape artist and could get out of anywhere. even the security lock on both front and back doors hadn't deterred her, and in the final attempt to keep her from leaving the house late at night to go to some gig or other, mum and dad had made her change bedrooms this time, without a drain pipe close to the window. Jemma paced the floor, Cortney, her friend had arranged to meet her. There was a great group playing in a large storage unit, probably unaware of the true owners of the property and Jemma was desperate to go.

She gazed out of the small window and sighed, (no drain pipe) there had to be some way she could escape the sanctuary of her prison. She leaned out of the window and examined her surroundings, there was a drain pipe a little distance from her window belonging to the neighbours next door, but too far away to reach by hand. What was she going to do? She sat on the bed and glanced round her room, there was nothing she could use. She paced the floor again, then giving up in anger, decided to go to bed. She threw her hold all on the floor which contained her clothes she had planned to wear, and tossed her bed covers back. Jemma stared at the bed, then smiled. A few minutes later, sheets were knotted together and draped down the wall from the bedroom window. Jemma climbed up on the window sill and climbed out the window gripping tight to the sheet in her hand. Jemma was a slender girl which allowed her to get out of small spaces, her long black hair complimented her very pretty face and of which was now tied in a bun out of the way. Jemma swung herself from side to side till she could reach the drainpipe of the next doors house and sliding down it, disappeared around the corner.

Mr and Mrs Jackson, were fully aware their children were out of control, but were powerless to stop them. Jemma at the age of seventeen did just what she wanted and had gone missing many a times unaware to her parents. Mr and Mrs Jackson settled in for the night. If they thought they knew where their daughter was, they had no idea what their son was doing. Nathan was nineteen and stood a good six feet in Hight, his blond slack curled hair shaggily hung to collar length, his curly fringe bordering his eyebrows. He had grown a thin beard and moustache in the hope it would make him look older, in fact it complimented his already handsome face. Nathan had disappointed his parents, he had studied hard and was excellent in mathematics, but had become bored with college and although great at problem solving, the idea of going on to university did not thrill him at all. No matter how hard his parents tried to persuade him, he didn't budge and in the end, dropped out of all education. Nathan drove up to his friend's house, they were heading to the casino, Gareth had been friends with Nathan all his life, but now at the age of twenty, had found himself a girlfriend and only went out with Nathan on the odd occasion. Gareth quickly put a comb through his black curly hair and grabbed his jacket off the peg, Nathan had come up with a system and was going to try it out on the roulette wheel, if it worked, they could be in for a lot of money.

Gareth jumped into the car, his very dark eyes gleaming as he thought of the money they may make. He glanced across at Nathan," you know, if we get caught we can be in a lot of trouble"; Nathan grinned, "is beating the system a crime" he replied; anyway, we won't get caught. The boys reached the casino and went inside. The casino was not that big, the slot machines filled a whole side of the room. The rest of the room was filled with the card table, bar, and of course the roulette table. Nathan and Gareth walked round the room, Nathan monitoring the moves of the card and roulette table. He had visited other casinos, but had only gained small amounts of money, but this casino played for large stakes and one had to be twenty-one to enter. Nathen finally played the roulette, he had worked out the next number and colour to win. Gareth crossed his fingers and held his breath as the little ball rolled round to a stop on the colour and number Nathan has picked. "Yes!" Gareth almost screamed, as the chips were pushed towards Nathan. By 3am the boys had won quite a lot of money and decided it was time to leave. "let's quit while we are ahead "Nathan quietly spoke; and made his way to the door, Gareth followed slowly behind him having another glance at the card table. He turned to look at Nathan and froze. Two big bouncers had grabbed Nathan on either arm and were walking him to the office Nathan quickly glanced at Gareth and slowly shook his head, indicating to Gareth, to do nothing. Gareth hung around for another hour, but on seeing Nathan escorted out the door and into a police car, he made his way to the car and went home.

Jemma Jackson, unaware of her brother's turmoil, was enjoying the music. "This is great "she shouted to Cortney; Cortney smiled and nodded, the music was too loud to talk. The girls walked the floor eyeing the boys and enjoying the attention they were getting back. "Got to go to the bathroom "Jemma yelled at Cortney; The girls made their way to a port a loo, but just as they reached the door, a yell came over the mike. "RAID, RUN!". The lock up became a danger zone as people ran to escape the police raid, Cortney getting dragged along with the crowd and splitting up from Jemma. Jemma, hid behind the port a loo, then when she had enough clear space, climbed out of a small window to the back of her and made her way down the long dark road to where a housing estate was situated followed close behind by more people and the police. She reached a corner house which was in Darkness, it didn't look like anyone was home. Jemma took off her heeled shoes and climbed over the garden gate. She could hear shouting and people running, and the sound of some- one climbing over the gate and looked around for a place to hide. There was a window high up, which looked like it could be the loft window. She looked around and sighed, "Yes" she thought to herself; As her eyes caught sight of a drain pipe. The pipe had a U bend in it, which made it easier to reach the window. Within a few seconds, Jemma had placed her shoes behind a shrub and was up the pipe. She entered the room which was in total darkness and sat on the floor under the window, waiting for the coast to clear. It seemed like an eternity for the hustle and bustle to cease, but finally everything calmed down and peace prevailed. 4am. The sky was getting brighter and Jemma had to be home before mam and dad got up. She peeped out of the window, all was quiet and the garden was empty. Maybe it was time to get out of here. She climbed out of the window and was just about to jump down from the pipe, when she was helped down by two police officers. Jemma sighed, mam and dad, were going to kill her.

Mr and Mrs Jackson, were fast asleep when a loud knock at the door woke them with a start. Mr Jackson jumped out of bed, "what the hell!", he exclaimed; He quickly ascended the stairs and opened the door to find a police man holding on to the arm of his son, and even worse, a police woman standing behind Jemma and guiding her through the door. Dave Jackson, stared at his daughter in disbelief, he looked ound the front door, trying to see how she had escaped. "How the? I don't believe!" he didn't get a chance to finish his words as the police walked through the door. Mrs Jackson, descended the stairs slowly, she was still half asleep. "what's going on?" she asked; Mr Jackson, indicated to the police and their children, "That's what is going on "he sighed; Mrs Jackson looked at her daughter "How did you get out of your bedroom?" she asked her daughter; "and what have you been up to?" she turned to her son.

PC Wilson, glanced across at Nathan. "Your son was spotted on security cameras, actually beating the system at a well know casino, brilliantly done I may say, but it is a crime and he is under age. After checking several casinos in nearby towns, it was discovered he had done the same there too, but had got away with it, until now. As for your daughter, she was at an illegal gig not too bad, however, to escape the police, she broke into a nearby house and was caught climbing out the window. Mr and Mrs Jackson, have you any control over your children?". Mr Jackson, sighed, and shook his head," apparently not" he exclaimed; He sadly looked across at his children when another knock came to the door. Mrs Jackson went to answer it and came back looking pale. "This is Mrs Brown, she is a social, worker" Mrs brown turned to the police officers. "I have been in touch with the station, and my office is taking on this case. Obviously, the children are out of control, but it is felt that sending them to a borstal institute or foster home, may not be the answer, we have a lady who runs a good correction facility, and will teach them how to use their abilities to get jobs and will bring them into line". Mrs Jackson, filled with tears, "I don't want them to go" she cried; Mrs brown softly smiled. "I know dear "she said; but if they don't, Jemma will go into care and Nathan may go to prison, this way, they can at least be together. Mr Jackson, put his arms round his wife. "Andrea, it's the best way, things can't go on like this" He turned to his children," you know that we love you both very much, this is the only way we can protect you now"; Jemma cried; she didn't want to go, but there was nothing she could do. Mrs Jackson packed some clothes for them both, and tearfully said good bye as the car owned by Mrs Brown, disappeared round the bend of the road.

Mrs Brown, glanced in her mirror at the young people she had in the back seat. "don't worry "she said; "things are not as bad as they seem, and your parents can come and see you every month". Nathan looked in the mirror back at her. "where are we going and how far is it?". Mrs Brown kept her eyes on the road. "The correction centre is in a remote location in the Yorkshire moors, we will be there in two hours". She replied; The car drove down winding roads and up steep hills, it seemed to take forever, then just when boredom and tiredness had set in, Mrs Brown took a sharp turn to the right and headed down a small country road which ended at the front of large iron gates. "Welcome to Chippingham House" she said; as the car slowly drove down a long drive and stopped in front of a large house which seemed to Jemma to look sad and lonely. Nathan and Jemma, went inside. There was a large square hall way, where a big oak door was situated at the right side of the hall, and a long passage to the left. Stairs led from the hall to a long passage both left and right of it and doors which looked like bedrooms lined both ways. Nathan, looked about him then looked at Jemma. He was just about to say something, when the large oak door opened and a lady in her fifties walked out, followed by a younger man, broad and muscly, Jemma would have said he had a great body, but right now, she didn't care.

Maddy Mason, walked over to the little group. "My name is Mrs Mason, I oversee this facility, and this is Trevor Howes my assistant, please follow me." She led them down the long passage and into a small office. Please sit down "she spoke; Mrs Brown, Jemma and Nathan, sat around her desk while she went through the rules and the reason they were there. Then they were led back to the hall way. "let me show you your rooms then come and meet the rest of the people here "she spoke; Nathan and Jemma were taken to their rooms which were basic, simply a bed, wardrobe, shower and TV. Jemma flung her bag on the bed as the door shut behind her, and sitting down near her bag, cried. Nathan, knocked at her door, "come on "He said; "We might as well see what's down stairs". Jemma dried her eyes and followed him down the stairs to the oak door. Nathan opened the door and followed by Jemma, walked in to a large room. Pool tables were placed at the back of the room, were a few boys were playing. A coffee and coke bar was to the right which was supervised, by what looked like a member of staff, as it was hard to tell who worked there, as no-one wore a uniform. Tables filled most of the room and there was a long window seat under the large window to the left which allowed light in and viewed panoramic scenery. Nathan and Jemma walked a little further into the room. "Everybody" Mrs Masons voice called out; "This is Nathan and Jemma, they are joining our group"; eyes all turned to give them the once over, then resumed whatever they were doing with disregard to who they were. "They will soon get use to you, "Mrs Mason smiled; "We usually have about fifty young people staying with us, but for now we only have forty, well! forty-two with yourselves". Nathan nodded and moved Jemma over to the window seat and was instantly ignored by the two girls who moved from where they were sitting. Jemma sat down, tears filling her eyes again. Nathan, put his hand round her arm, "don't worry!" He whispered; We are not staying"; Jemma stared back at him. When Nathan said something, he usually meant it. "What do you have in mind?" She asked; Nathan glanced round the room. "There are cameras all over the place, but you can get out of anywhere, what we need to do, is check the place out, see were the weaknesses are then plan our move" He replied; Jemma nodded. "How long do you think it will take us" she asked; Nathan sighed; "I don't know for sure, we don't know what is round the grounds. Probably about two or three weeks, you will just have to be patient, we are going to have to pretend to settle in and check the place out, then make our move". Jemma, brightened up. Now she knew they wouldn't be staying, she could cope with what had to be done.

Liam Denver sat in the back of his friend, Jamie, car. Jamie had gone to a girlfriend house while her parents were out, but they had returned early, had gone to bed and had locked the door behind them. Jamie had climbed out of the bedroom window, but had discovered that both garden gates were locked too. He would have tried to climb the wall, but barbed wire hung from the top, to hopefully keep any unsociable people out, and in the end, had to call Liam who could pick any lock. Liam, quietly made his way to the front gate. He wasn't very happy, he had to walk a mile to the house and he didn't have a car. Jamie, stood by the gate," Have you got it open yet?" He asked; Liam sighed, "Yes! Its open" He replied; Jamie opened the gate, but unfortunately for him, the gate had a loud creek, and woke the house hold up. Jamie and Liam made a run for it, Liam, heads in front, as they ran down the long road and turned the corner to the welcoming sight of Jamie car. Liam waited for Jamie to open it and dived into the back seat. Jamie turned his head to look at Liam and smiled, "That was close" He exclaimed; Liam sighed, all he wanted to do was to go home.

Liam sat in his bedroom, at eighteen, all he was interested in, was going for a drink, and playing on his X Box. He was a handsome lad, with short dark brown hair which was parted to the left and of which strands would hang over his eye. He was growing a beard and moustache, and his brother Ashley, would often comment that he looked like Shaggy, off Scooby doo. Liam and Ashley, argued on many occasion, and one could make the mistake that they were not close. In fact, the boys were very close and would confide in each other, much to the annoyance of their mother who was the last to know anything. Mrs Denver, raised the boys on her own, and the boys adored her. However, the boys had to be left alone on many occasions, as Julie Denver had to work to support them. It was during these times that both boys had found themselves an interest. Liam, took up magic, and learned very quickly how to unlock the puzzles and had gone on to try his hand at proper locks. It was because of this, that he learned that he could undo any lock except a combination lock, and friends intended to use him for many reasons, one, "for getting friends out of their girlfriend's bedrooms". Liam was playing on his game when his phone rang. Friends were asking him to go out. Mam had already gone to work and wouldn't be back till midnight. Ashley was out too, he had gone to play football. Liam sighed, he was happy on his game, but it beat being in the house on his own. He put on his good jeans and top and hoped he had enough money in his bank to buy his drinks. Liam walked through the doors of the pub to find Jammie and a few friends sitting round a couple of tables. Jamie beckoned to him to come over he had that fed up look on his face. "What's the matter?" Liam asked; Jamie frowned," one of the lads had organised a party at his house, his parents were going away for the week-end, but there had been a problem and they had to cancel and were staying home he replied; "What's worse", one of the lads but in; "Is that he's invited thirty people". Liam cringed, "what are you going to do?" He asked; The boy who was giving the party shook his head, "Don't know!" he replied; Not unless we can get into my dad's warehouse." Jamie, looked at the boy, "will your dad let us use it?" He asked; "Hell No, but as long as its cleaned up, he won't know" He replied; everyone looked at each other, "No good" The lad sighed; "He keeps it double locked"; Jamie looked across at Liam, Liam frowned, he knew what he was going to ask. The group of boys lowered their heads "can you do it?" Jamie asked; The boys stared at Liam. Liam looked round at their eager expressions. "I don't know, probably" He replied; "That's settled" Jamie smiled; "I will drop you off at the warehouse, you can unpick the locks and the rest of us will go and get the word out where to come and pick some of the girls up"; Liam sighed but nodded, there was nothing he could do except punch Jamie in the nose, later.

Liam found himself standing outside the warehouse doors, "Two locks "He thought to himself. "One low down and the other further up the door". At 5ft 11 inch, Liam didn't find the height of the second lock a problem. He set to and began unlocking the first lock, "Good "He thought, "One lock down, one to go. He bent on one knee and began to unlock the second lock, when he was grabbed from behind and pulled to his feet. Liam turned sharply round hoping to escape the clutches of his aggressors only to find his arms were forced behind his back and handcuffed. Liam tried to struggle, but his slender frame, couldn't compare to the bulk and size of the officers. Liam was pushed inside the police car, the only thing going through his mind (was that his mother was going to kill him). Liam sat back in his seat, something sharp had dug into his wrist, it was one of the tools he had used to open the locks which he had stuffed up his sleeve when the police had caught him. Liam gently pulled it out, if he could unlock the handcuffs, he could make a run for it. The police car pulled up outside the station, Liam got out of the back seat he had escaped the cuffs and now, pushing passed the officers, ran. Unfortunately for Liam, two other officers were just coming out of the station and on seeing what had happened, caught him before he had a chance to get to far. Liam was escorted into the station and placed in a cell. The door was bolted and the officers walked away still carrying the handcuffs, "Well, he won't escape from there!" one officer said; "yes" replied the other; But he is bloody good!".

Ashley Denver, was playing football on the football field, unaware of his brother's trouble. He and his friends had been chased away from near his home after hitting one or two cars with the football. At the age of sixteen, Ashley was nearly as tall as his brother and stood a good 5ft8inch. His light brown hair, was styled and groomed, and would often be called a chav by Liam, and just like Liam was of slender build. Ashley was sporty and very quick on his feet and wasn't easy to catch. Ashley, played on for a while then called it a night. A few of his friends walked back with him, they were a rowdy lot and Ashley secretly hoped that they wouldn't have done. The small group walked down the street throwing pebbles at each other and hitting windows and cars in the process. Ashley hurried passed Hoping to get away from them, but they followed on. Ashley cut down a back lane passing some shops (the quickest way home). The boys ran after him laughing and jumping around until one lad threw a large stone which ended up going through a shop window. Ashley turned to see, he could hear police sirens in the background, the lads took off, leaving Ashley on his own. He looked about him. Police officers were coming towards him, Ashley ran with the police on his heels. The officers chased him down the street, but Ashley left them standing, he ran towards a housing estate and through the streets and headed towards another bloc of shops, he darted down a back alleyway and hid there for a while. Half an hour had gone by, and all seemed quiet. Ashley sneaked out from the alley way and head towards home. He was almost there when a police car pulled up behind him. Again, he took to his heels, as a second car arrived, and ran off at top speed, if they caught him he would go down for criminal damage, even though he hadn't done anything, he was there. He picked up pace and once again, left the police standing. How- ever, unfortunately for Ashley, a third car had arrived, and following instructions, had circled round cutting Ashley's escape route off. Ashley couldn't do anything but give up, and fifteen minutes later, arrived at the same police station as Liam.

Liam Denver, was led from the cells and was escorted to the interview room, as Ashley walked through the door. He had just been to the desk to be signed in and was also on his way to the interview room. Both boys passed each other and turning their heads sharply round, stared at each other. "What are you doing here!" They both said; at the same time. The officer with Liam frowned, "So, you both know each other"; Liam said nothing. "This is Ashley Denver, the officer in charge of Ashley spoke to the other officer; "And this is Liam Denver" the other officer replied; as he led Liam to the interview room. Ashley too was escorted to a room were both boys were questioned. Liam sat in a chair, as another officer came into the room and set up the recorder. Liam explained what had happened and signed his statement. "What will happen now?" Liam asked; The officer looked at him. "One of your friends has come forward and verified your story, How-ever, the owner of the lock up, still says you were braking in and is still pressing charges. This means you will still be charged with breaking and entering and a court date will be set". Liam felt sick, he didn't want to go to prison.

Ashley, walked into the interview room and was told to sit down. He explained what had happened, and that he hadn't done anything and signed his statement. He too, asked what would happen to him, he was shaking and frightened and the officer in charge could tell, this wasn't a bad lad. "Sadly," He spoke; you will be charged with criminal damage. You may not have thrown the stones or kicked the ball, but you were there. The security camera from the shop picked only you up, and you were the only one there when police were called, and only you who ran!". Ashley's eyes, filled with tears, he only wanted to go home. As the interview finished, an officer entered the room and whispered something in the other officer's ears. "Your mother is here" the interviewing officer turned to Ashley. "Come on, I will take you to her". Liam and Ashley were taken to a waiting room, where Mrs Denver, and another lady was waiting. Ashley and Liam put their arms round her neck and hugged her. "What have you been doing both of you?" She asked; "It's not as it seems mam!" But they are going to charge us anyway" Liam complained; Ashley gripped his mother, he was still shaking, "They say we might have to go to prison!" He sadly spoke; Mrs Denver, stroked her boys head, "This is Mrs Brown," She said softly; "She is a social worker, and has come to help". The boys looked across at her. "Mrs Brown said there is a correction facility in the Yorkshire dales. I can phone you twice a week and visit every month. If you go and serve the time, all charges will be cleared and you won't have to go to prison". She continued; The boys looked over to where Mrs Brown stood, they didn't want to go, but right now, anything sounded better than prison. The boys signed the acceptance form, and Mrs Denver handed them a small suit case full of some of their clothes. "You have to go now," She explained; "but I will be with you in thought every day and will phone you as soon as I am allowed"; Mrs Brown, led the boys to her car and turned to Mrs Denver. I will ring you with the days you can call the boys, and the visiting date. We just ask that you give the boys a few weeks to settle in". Mrs Denver nodded, and tearfully watched her boys been driven away. She walked back to her car and getting in, cried like a baby. Two hours later, Mrs Browns car turned down the dirt track road which led to the great iron gates of Chippingham and entered the large hallway where the boys were introduced to Mrs Mason and Trevor Howes. They were shown to their rooms and left to unpack and told to come down and meet every-one. Liam unpacked and went to Ashley's room. Ashley was Sitting on his bed. He had been crying and hadn't unpacked.

Liam put his clothes away for him and sat next to him. "let's go and see what is down stairs" he encouragingly spoke; Ashley nodded and dried his eyes, then followed Liam down stairs and through the big oak door. Eyes looked at them and Mrs Mason came over and introduced them to every-one. Liam and Ashley looked about them, (What a place!). Liam led Ashley to a distant table in a far corner and they sat down." We are not going to like it here are we" Ashley turned to Liam; "I don't think so" He said; Liam looked about him, groups of boys were looking over and laughing, Liam stared back, for all the boys quiet demur, they had been to kick boxing and were not the push overs the other boys thought. "Let's give it a week or two, to show mam we tried, then we are leaving". Ashley looked at Liam and for the first time that day gave a slight smile. "Good" He said; "Good";

Nazi Weza, sat in her room. She was a very pretty African girl with long braids in her hair. She had come to England to live with her father at the age of twelve, and now at the age of nineteen she had qualifications in Travel and Tourism and a diploma in I.T, and was a wiz with the computer. Naz spent most of her time in her room. Dad worked and spent most of his time going out. His wife had died some years back and he was now dating on a regular basis. This meant Naz was left alone, her only companion was her computer. Naz spoke to many people on line, but she also played the odd game or two, and on a couple of occasions had broken down and deciphered hidden channel or locked doors. Most of what she down loaded, was porn, dating, gambling, and a special kind of dating service. Naz wasn't interested in any of them, her thrill was just braking the code. Naz sat at her computer and entered the rooms of locked doors. "Which one should I choose She thought; She looked through the doors and noticed one door didn't seem the same as the others, she pressed enter and the door swung open. She stared at the screen as (PASSWORD) appeared. "Now what could that be!" she grinned; and entered all the usual passwords. "Nothing!" She thought. She tried several more passwords, but nothing was happening. Naz thrived on this, this was a challenge and the more she couldn't get through, the more she wanted to try. She sat and pondered the problem. "This is not a normal password" She spoke out loud; She sat back and stared at the screen. "Hum!" She moaned; "Some passwords are not names, I wonder if it's just letters?" she spoke to herself; She glanced at the password name and began to type different letters. She went through the alphabet till she reached N. The letter bounced to life on the screen. "Now we are getting somewhere". She smiled; She typed in more, and went right through the alphabet till she reached X. Again, the letter jumped out of the screen at her, she continued, but nothing happened. "Damn!" She moaned; "most passwords have about eight to ten digits" She complained; "I can only get two". She went through the alphabet again till she reached the letter L. "N X L" She sighed; She went through the alphabet several times, but to no avail. She sat back in her chair, (this wasn't going to be easy!". She had exhausted the alphabet, what else could she do. She sat and pondered the situation, maybe numbers followed. She went through all the logical numbers, but still nothing. She slammed her hand down on the key board hitting the o button as she did so. To her surprise, the o appeared on the screen. She stared in disbelief, "Is this a binary code?" She exclaimed; She pressed the 1 button, the 1 appeared. Naz tried several different sequins until, finally, the code was complete. "It's done," she boasted; And in anticipation pressed the enter button. The screen sprang to life, but what she saw, confused her. It looked like a plan of a strange building which resembled a dome. The dome looked like it covered the whole of the British Isles, and seemed to have its base three miles out, deep at the bottom of the ocean. The dome was sectioned out with what looked like holding ports for ships or subs. These holding ports were based at each end of the country and in the centre, more sections were formed. Naz stared in disbelief, (What was she looking at!). She rolled the screen around till in the very top corner, she saw the words (TOP SECRET). Naz closed the door down instantly, this was hush hush, stuff, and she didn't want any part of that. Naz, was about to close her computer down, when a crashing sound came from down stairs, the next she knew, was that several armed police were standing in her room and her computer confiscated. Naz, was taken from her room by force and placed in the back of a large van. Several minutes later, she was dragged from the van and placed in a room.

Naz, sat in the room, she was very frightened and in tears, she didn't know what was happening, or where she was. Several minutes later, the door opened and a man walked through. He sat down in a chair opposite her, and stared at her. "Well Miss Weza! Do you know why you have been brought here?". Naz, looked back at him through tear filled eyes. "Because I Saw something I shouldn't" She replied; "Exactly "The man replied; "So what are you? a terrorist, spy, traitor". Naz looked in horror, her eyes widening allowing the water in them to roll down her cheek. "None of that she exclaimed; "Then why did you go on the site, open the door and break the code". He enquired; his voice raised with a slight tone of aggression. Naz raised her head and shrugged. "Because I can, "She replied; The man looked at her, then picking up his file from the desk, walked out of the room, still not telling her, who he was. Naz, sat back in the chair, it was 2 am, and she was feeling lonely, worried, and with all the crying, very tired. It seemed to take forever, before the man came back into the room. "Miss Weza, you will be tried for hacking and possibly spying, that will be up to the judge". Naz cried, she may have broken the code, but she hadn't meant anything by it. "follow me please" he spoke; Gesturing her to leave the room. Naz stood up and was about to leave, when another man came in and whispered something to her interrogator. Naz was told to sit back down as both men left the room. Ten minutes later, the man came back. "Well, well" he exclaimed; "We have a Mrs Brown outside, she's a social worker, and is working with our department. This could be your lucky day, she is willing to take you to a correction centre instead of prison. They will work with you and hopefully, rehabilitate you, but you will have to sign an agreement form". Naz, so happy not to go to prison, agreed to sign the form. "Mrs Brown will take you there now, and will inform your family of what has happened and pick you up some clothes". He informed her and took her out and introduced her to Mrs Brown. Naz, walked through the doors of chippingham and was introduced to Mrs Mason and Trever Howes, who took her to her room instructing her that her alarm would go off at 9am and to go to the room through the oak door where she would have breakfast and be introduced to the rest of the young people there. Naz was exhausted, and fell asleep almost at once. 9am, the alarm went off, and Naz dressed and made her way to the oak door. She hesitated, but knowing there was nowhere to go, entered. She looked about her, as Mrs Mason came over and introduced her to the large group, who barely looked up, they were too interested in the breakfast which had just been brought in. Naz was shown to a table, but didn't eat anything. She was heartbroken and looking round the dismal room, knew she wouldn't be staying there.

CHAPTER TWO

Jemma Jackson, sat on her bed. Tears were beginning to form in her eyes. She had been at Chippingham House for two weeks now and Nathan, her brother, still hadn't come up with a plan to go. She wiped her eyes, and walked out of her little room as Nathan left his. He could see she had been crying and knew he had to come up with something, soon. They made their way to the pool room and opened the oak door. The pool tables were already in use, but the patio doors behind the tables had been opened to let in air and allow the teens to sit in a small garden. Nathan led Jemma to the garden. Jemma sat in silence, she was home sick and hated Chippingham. Nathan looked about him, cameras were everywhere. "No wonder no-one ran" He thought to himself, "they would be picked up before they left the house". He went to fetch Jemma a coke and a bag of crisps it would occupy her for the time being. He sat down stretching his legs out and putting his arms at the back of his head. He stared into the beautiful blue clear sky deep in thought. Jemma put her head on his arm, she knew he was doing all he could. The two sat there, their only thoughts were of how to escape. How long they would have sat there, wasn't known, as their peace was disturbed by a pigeon almost hitting Nathan on the head and then finding a perch on top of one of the cameras. Nathan stared at the pigeon "Bloody Bird!" he thought, then in an instant looked across at Jemma. He looked across at the other cameras his mind racing. "What's wrong!" Jemma asked; Nathan, smiling turned to her. "We need feathers" He replied;

Jemma stared back "Say What!" She exclaimed; Had her brother gone mad. Nathan, nodded to the pigeon. "No-one will take any notice if a pigeon lands on the cameras they will wait till it has flown off. If we could pick up the loose feathers and tie them together and drape them over the cameras, it would give us coverage to get out of the garden and down towards that wall" He nodded to the wall which stood behind the garden wall and across a green field. "I have been watching the cameras" He explained; "There is a blank spot, as the cameras move round in opposite directions, they don't quite meet in the middle and has created a bland spot. If we can cover one camera with the feathers, it will give us a chance to reach the blind spot and over the wall". Jemma, hugged her brother, "You're a genius" She laughed; Nathan gave his sister a slight hug back, it was nice to see her happy again.

Liam and Ashley Denver, also made their way to the garden. Nathan looked at them as they entered and nodded. Liam nodded back, but neither spoke. Ashley sat on the seat and twiddled his thumbs. "When are we going to get away?" He asked; Liam, put his head down "Don't talk to loud," Liam whispered back," Every-one will hear you!". Ashley, put his head down, he couldn't take much more. Liam, sighed. if he didn't do something, Ashley would run. Mam was expecting him to take care of Ashley. He looked about him also noticing the cameras, "How was he going to do it!". He looked around the garden and noticed the cameras turned at alternative times, "If the cameras at the front did the same, he could jam the bracket to slow down the movement of one camera, while dodging the second. This would give Ashley time to run the path to the front gate and jam a camera there, giving them both a chance to climb the gate and escape. He turned to Ashley," putting his head close to his "I think I've found our way out," He whispered; Ashley slightly lifted his head, "You have?" He whispered back; Liam nodded," but you will have to run like the wind". He explained what his plan was and what was needed to be done. Ashley, grinned Got it!".

Naz Weza, sat alone at a table in the pool room. Most of the group were in the garden, but she didn't want to be near them. She was still there when Nathan and Jemma Jackson walked through, on their way back to Nathan's room, followed late by Liam and Ashley Denver, as they made their way to Liam's room. Naz, was lonely, she hadn't mixed with any-one 'she didn't want to' but this isolated her, making her feel even more vulnerable. She sat with her coke and sighed. She needed to get out of here, 'but how!'. Everywhere had a camera, everywhere except Mrs Mason's room. If she could get in there, she could climb out of her window, there were bushes and trees at that side and although her room was on the top floor, she could climb down the tree and get over the wall, then make her way to the wall which led to freedom. Naz, had never stopped looking for a way out since the day she had arrived. Her bedroom was only a few doors from the stairs and from her window in her room she could see round the side of the garden. Mrs Mason's room was at the right side of the house around the corner of the side garden and Naz caught a glance of a tree branch, indicating a tree was there. Cameras were situated on each corner of the left and right wall, but when the camera on the right turned to look down the side garden, a black spot was formed and Naz believed if she could dodge the camera by climbing the tree she could then get on the garden wall and on to the grounds behind it. She had no idea, what she was going to do when she reached the gate, or how she was going to dodge the camera's and her main problem was how she was going to get the key away from Mrs Mason. She had monitored Mrs Masons movements for over a week, and had noticed that she kept her key in her trouser pocket, but how was she going to get it out of there. She sat back on her chair as a group of boys came through the door. "Let's have a look" one of the boys called out to a ginger haired lad of about sixteen. The boy held something out in his hand. "Is it strong?" the boy asked again "Watch" the lad with the ginger hair spoke; and held out a magnet which he pointed at a folk on the table, the folk instantly jumped off the table and clung to the magnet." Wicked!" He exclaimed; "Fantastic!" Naz thought to herself, if she could sweet talk the boy, maybe he would lend her it then she could use it to get the key from Mrs Masons pocket. The boys left the room, now followed by Naz, for now, she would go to her room and plan.

Every-one had come in from the garden now and the patio doors were closed and locked. Two of the assistants remained in the room, While Mrs Mason and a few of her assistants had been called to her office. "What's the matter Chris?" she asked; Chris Carson oversaw the camera's and checked them regularly. He had been monitoring every-one in the garden. "I think you may be interested in this" He told her. He slipped the disc into the computer as all eyes turned to the screen. The camera had picked up the group in the garden it had also caught Nathan and Jemma quietly whispering to each other and Nathans interest in his surroundings. The camera had also focused on Liam and Ashley's conversation. Mrs Mason frowned, it looked as if they are planning to run, best keep an eye on them ". Chris Carson, nodded, "I don't know if this is important but if you look". He moved the disc on till it reached Naz in the pool room, "It doesn't seem much, but." He broke off and allowed Mrs Mason to judge for herself. The camera picked the boys out and Naz, her eyes glued to the magnet in the boy's hand and the pleasure in her eyes. "I think it's very important" she sighed; She turned to Trever Howe's, "I think we are going to have to bring things closer" She said; "Organise it Trever!". Trever Howe's nodded and left the room. Mrs Mason Looked at every-one, "Now it begins".

The next day, the sun shone, the sky was blue and clear with only a few white puffy clouds. The group entered the room to have breakfast. Mrs Mason, waited till they had eaten then addressed them. "We are taking you all on an outing," she spoke; "It's to an indoor zoo, not much I know, but it will get you out of Chippingham for a while". Votes of 'yeh!' went around the room, but not every-one was happy. "It is 9-30am, I would like you all to go to your rooms and get a coat, then meet me in the hall at 11am!" Mrs Mason continued; The group went to their rooms and at 11am congregated in the hall. Trever Howe's, stood in the hall with a list in his hand, "We can't all go in together!" He spoke; "So I have placed you all in groups of ten except for one who will have five in it. When I call your name, I want you to get into your group. you can sit were- ever you like on the bus but once we arrive you will get into your group". The bus pulled away from Chippingham, and headed deep into the country side, an hour and a half later, the bus pulled in to a large estate. The drive way to the lodge was long and bordered by trees hiding the grounds behind them. The rolling hills, were thick with greenery and behind the lodge just behind more hills, was the sea which looked like it was in line with the land. The lodge was beautiful with a thatched roof, its windows were large and a large white door, guarded the entrance giving it a proper rural look. Every-one got off the bus and was guided in their groups. Mrs Mason got out of her car, she had followed the bus down. "Right!" She said; Group one, follow me." She led the group down a long corridor and through large doors at the end of it. The rest of the groups had been taken into a games room which harboured pool tables and which would entertain them till each group had finished.

Naz Weza was in group one, she followed the other members of her group until, they reached large thick glass doors. The glass doors were opened by remote control and the group walked in. Naz looked around her, she was standing in what looked like a huge factory floor, which spread for miles. Large thick glass doors were spaced round it like a half horseshoe and beyond that, a huge pool. The group went through the first glass doors and found themselves standing in a field. Trees were scattered here and there and she could hear noise coming from further over the field. She stood still. She didn't particularly want to come and she wasn't that fond of animals. She walked a little way further but kept the doors with in eye view. Three of the girls who were in the group, looked over at her and laughed. 'Don't know why she would be frightened, she should be at home here' one of the girls cruelly spoke; Naz glared back at her but said nothing and watched as the rest of the group moved on. Suddenly, one of the boys gave a shout," Look! Chimps" he exclaimed; The group watched in awe as chimps swung from branch to branch. "Don't worry" a voice behind them said; "The animals are trained and won't harm you". Chris Carter, was part of the team at Hillock which was the name of the lodge, he had followed the group in to supervise them. The group walked over to where the chimps were, but as they closed in, the chimps moved. Some of the boys tried to get close again, but the chimps were not interested and swung from branch to branch, tree to tree. Chris Carter, sighed;" Let's move on there is more animals to see in the next unit". He turned to go and stopped. He looked at Naz who had refuse to move to far from the door and gazed up at the tree above her head. The chimps had moved round and were now sitting in the tree that naz stood under. "They must have smelt you!" the same girl that had insulted her before laughed; Naz just put her head down, 'She hated that girl'. The group walked towards her and headed for the door, Naz staid were she was till they passed. "Are You stopping there, Weza?" one of the lads called to her, as the group headed for the door then turned to look at her to see her response. But to their surprise, the chimps had jumped down from the tree and were standing behind her. Naz, on seeing the look on the groups faces, turned to look behind her then froze. The chimps were sitting on the ground just behind her, their eyes glued on the group. Naz, put one foot slowly forward, then another. "what time's Christmas?" another lad called out. Naz took another step. "are you coming or what?" the girl who had insulted her spoke; as she took a step forward. At this, the chimps got to their feet, and Naz found a hairy hand in hers. The group stared as Naz stood hand in hand with the chimp surrounded by the rest. Chris Carter straightened up, his blue eyes shining and walked towards her. Naz was shaking, "Come on!" He said; "You come with me". He walked her to the door and guided her through. Mrs Mason was standing near the big doors where they had first come in and looked over at Chris Carter, Chris Carter looked back and put a finger up, Mrs Mason slightly nodded as Naz was taken to a Miss Goodall. "Miss Goodall, will take you to a room where you can pull round". Chris Carter turned to Naz. "She will take care of you". Barbara Goodall, took Naz by the arm, "come with me dear let's get you comfortable!". She said; Barbara Goodall was in her early forties she wasn't beautiful, but was pretty and carried her age well. Miss Goodall glanced across at Chris Carter and nodded. Chris Carter, walked off to bring the next group in as the first group moved on. Chris Carter was in his late to early thirties. His dark brown hair, complimented his deep blue eyes giving him a ruggedly handsome look which most of the girls had noticed. As the group moved off without her, Naz was shown into a large dining area and was placed at a table where she was given crisps and a bottle of coke to drink. Naz looked about her, Barbara Goodall had made her excuse saying she would be back soon as she had to see to the second group and had left her on her own.

The second group had now been escorted through the doors and were taken over to the chimp area. Liam Denver, was in the second group, much to the annoyance of his brother Ashley. Liam walked into the chimp field but didn't go too far in, he was worried about his brother. The rest of the group walked on leaving him by his self and walked over to where the chimps were sitting in the trees. Liam backed further to the doors 'This wasn't for him!'. As the group got closer, the chimps moved away, one or two of them had made their way to the tree Liam was standing next to and cocking their heads, looked at him. Liam headed for the doors and waited outside. Shortly after, the group returned and headed for the next area 'Coward!' one of the boys whispered to another boy. Liam ignored it, he just wanted to get back to Ashley. The large glass door opened and the group were escorted in by Chris Carter. Liam slowly walked in 'What now!' he thought to himself; The field he was standing in was huge, and Chris Carter was explaining something to the group, but Liam wasn't listening. The group walked further on, the land seemed to go on forever. He slowly followed the group over a small hill and stood at the top while the rest of the group walked on. The group headed towards a patch of thickly dense woodland of which from it, walked two elephants. Liam froze, and turning around, walked slowly back down the hill. The group stood in awe as the elephants walked away from them and headed in Liam's direction. The elephants, walked round the hill and out of sight of the group who couldn't believe their eyes, Chris Carter, moved them on. "make your way to the doors "He called to the group. The group went back over the hill passing Liam as they went 'What a pussy!' a lad spoke to another lad. Liam looked back at the boy," I'm not the only one" he replied'; If this lad wanted a fight he would give him one. The boy took a step forward as Liam also took a step forward. Chris Carter walked in between the two boys then stopped. Liam stood there his fist clenched, when he suddenly felt something blowing in his hair, he unclenched his fist and brushed his hair with his hand. Every-one stood still and held their breath. Once again, he felt something blowing in his ear and went to brush it away with his hand, but his hand felt something dry and rough. Liam grabbed it and slowly turning around, looked in shock at the trunk which lay in his hand. Liam instantly dropped it, but the elephant lifted his trunk, and rubbed it against his head. Liam was white and backed slowly away. Chris Carter, walked forward and took Liam by the arm. "Come with me!" He spoke; and led him out the door. Mrs Mason, saw Liam with Chris Carter, Chris Carter, looked over to Mrs Mason and put up two of his fingers. Mrs Mason nodded, now for group three. Liam was taken over to Barbara Goodall, and was escorted to the room Naz sat in. Liam sat at the same table and was also given crisps and coke. He sat down still shaken and white, Naz looked over at him "Are you alright?" She asked; Liam nodded, 'he was now!'. He sat silently, his feet stretched out his hand gripping the coke bottle. Miss Goodall, smiled "I will leave you both for the time being, I am just going to assist the third group and at that, she left the room.

The third group went through the door and stood in front of the first large glass doors as the first group were escorted out of the building and into the grounds and the second group headed further on. Jemma stood at the back of the group. Connie Gibb, the girl Jemma hated, was in her group, the further away she was from her, the better. Jemma stood at the doorway, she wasn't going to follow the group. One of the chimps looked down from a branch of a tree and looked at her, but Jemma didn't want to know. The group came out and headed for the next glass door. Jemma once again stood at the doorway Connie Gibb constantly passing sarcastic comments at her. Jemma was getting more and more angry. The group came out and went to the third door Jemma again getting comments from Connie. Once again, she stayed near the door, she wished that Nathan was with her. She looked round at Chris Carter who nodded to her to go in. This time Jemma went in. She walked further into the field which was filled with long grass and shrubs, there was nothing in sight. She walked further in fighting her way through the grass which reached her waist and found herself standing on shorter grass which stretched for quite a distance. Jemma stopped, this was as far as she was going. The group went further on and stopped when a loud roar filled the air and from round the shrubs came a lion. Even the group backed off, but Chris Carter, spoke to them and they stood still. Jemma was too far away to hear what he had said and she didn't really care. The lion walked away from the group and looked across the field at Jemma "Oh crap!" she said out loud; and ran back through the long grass to were the door was situated. The group made their way back and shook their head at Jemma. Connie Gibb, smirked over at her, "What's the matter Jackson? Frightened of pussy cats!"; Jemma glared back. Connie Gibb, looked over at her," I don't know why you came!" She taunted; "You have spent most of the time sitting at the doorway, 'Coward'. Jemma had enough, "I didn't want to be with you "she replied;" You are a pain in the backside". Connie Gibb walked over to her "And you are a freak!" she shouted back; Jemma took a step towards her, "And you only think your good" Jemma shouted back; Connie Gibb, put her face near Jemma's "How would you like a punch in the face!" she threatened; Jemma. "How would you like me to put you down!" Jemma threatened back. Chris Carter, tried to push his way through the group which had now gathered round to see the argument, 'This was a useless group' he thought to himself. He managed to get to the front just as Connie Gibb raised her fist, but Jemma pounced, and landed a blow on Connie's jaw. Connie Gibb, went to the floor, and was helped up by her friends. They stood with her, ganging up on Jemma, when they stopped and backed off. Two of the lions, on hearing the commotion, had come to investigate and had now stood at either side of Jemma eyeing the group as they did so. Chris Carter, slowly shook his head, 'I don't believe it' he thought to himself, 'Who would of thought 'Her!'. He told the group to go through the door and went over to Jemma. "Come on Mohammed Ali" He grinned; "Let's get your hand treated it looks swollen." Jemma, didn't move, the lions were still by her side and she was terrified. "They won't hurt you," Carter talked to her; "Just take a step forward." Jemma shacking stepped forward her legs were trembling and felt like jelly. The big cats turned and moved off. Jemma took another step, then another finally reaching the door and fell through it, helped by Chris Carter. "Come with me "he spoke; Miss Goodall will take you to a place where you can calm down and get that hand seen too". Jemma was handed over to Barbara Goodall and was led though the door that led to the dining room to join the others. He walked back to see the fourth group in and put three fingers up at Mrs Mason.

Jemma, stared at the trio who sat round the table and sat down with them while Barbara Goodall went to get her something to eat and drink and a cold compress for her hand. "Are you alright?" Naz asked her; Jemma nodded, her eyes streaming with tears, 'Where was Nathan?'. Naz went to get her some tissues which were placed on a far side table and brought her some over. Jemma took them from her and smiled "Thank you" She said; and wiped her eyes. Liam looked at her hand, "That's quite a bruise you have there" He exclaimed. "Who did you hit to get that?". Jemma grinned, "Connie Gibb," she said; Liam nodded, "right, if there is one person that needs a slap, it's her" He replied; They sat in silence for a while, no-one knowing quite what to say. Liam looked round the room and back at the girls. Naz, glanced at him. "Something isn't right, is it!" She whispered; Liam shook his head, "No!" he whispered back, "Where are all the others?". Jemma looked across at them, "How did you get here?" she asked; Naz sighed." Just like you, I was getting verbal abuse, we were in the chimp field and one of the girls was having a go at me because I didn't go right in. She was getting really aggressive, when a chimp came up and held my hand, I was petrified, all the chimps were standing behind me, when Mr Carter, came over and took me out." Liam frowned; "That's like what happened to me. You know how these lot are, they have had a go at us since the minute we came, it's almost like we have disturbed their little group. I didn't want to go to see the animals to start with, so when we were near the chimp field, I remained back and didn't go in. of course I got called by the lads, so when we reached the next door, I went in. 'that place is huge!' I went as far as a hill then saw an elephant. I didn't go any further.

I froze for a second or two, then ran back to the door, elephants were just a bit too much. The group came back and I got more criticism. I was going to head for the door, when I felt a kind of breeze blowing my hair, I brushed it off, but something blew in my ear. I grabbed hold of it and turned around, I was holding the trunk of an elephant. I couldn't move, so Chris Carter, came and brought me here." Jemma stared at them both. "That's weird!" she exclaimed; "I didn't want to see the animals and didn't want to go in, Connie Gibb, was picking on me and I was really sick of her so didn't want to go near her. Finally, I went in this door but as soon as I saw the lions, I ran back to the door,' I mean lions, for crying out loud, there was no way I was staying there. Connie Gibb caught me at the door, that's when I punched her, her friends came to her rescue, but by then two of the lions had stood by my side, I fell to pieces and was brought here." The trio stared at each other, 'What was going on!' these were not ordinary animals, what was this place? and what were they up too!

The fourth group entered. Ashley was part of that group. He too, was not interested, all he wanted to do was get back to Liam. The group went from room to room. Ashley refused to go in. They came to the forth room. "Ashley, are you going in this time?" Chris Carter asked; Ashley, looked at him looking very forlorn. The door opened and Ashley walked in. Chris Carter, led the group far into the field. The grass was short and rocks covered some of the ground. Far in the distance, a rocky hill was formed and a cave. Ashley walked a little further, 'What was going to be in this place' he thought to himself. He glanced back at the door, he had gone further in than he wanted to be and was some way from the door for comfort. He stopped, he wasn't going any further. The group walked on then stopped as a Cheetah came out from the cave, followed by another. Ashley stared in disbelief, 'Oh flip!' he exclaimed; and took to his heals, he would feel a lot safer nearer the door. A few minutes later, the group came back. Ashley walked towards the door and stood behind the line of boys. Some looked at him and tutted, Ashley took no notice. Chris Carter, looked round the group, he seemed disappointed. The line of boys went down and Ashley found himself standing were two trees were placed. He moved down one place standing in between the two trees. 'Come on' he thought to himself, he just wanted to get out of there. He sighed, it seemed to take forever. He stood watching the line go down when he felt something touching his hair. He brushed it aside, no-one dared touch his hair. He stood a few seconds more, and again something touched his hair. Ashley put his hand on his head and felt a heavy weight land on his hand. He looked up and nearly fainted, as a cheetah placed its paw on his hand. Ashley turned white and backed away, he turned hoping to make a dash for the door, but a long tail dropped from the second tree baring his way. Ashley tried to dodge the tail when a head poked out from the leaves, and he found himself face to face with another cheetah. Ashley could feel the tears well in his eyes, he was frightened, these were wild cats. He began to tremble, when the cat leaned forward and a wet tongue licked his face. Chris Carter, nodded and smiled. He went over to him and putting his arm around him, led him to the door. "Come on" he spoke; "Let me take you to Liam." Ashley walked through the doors of the dining room and on seeing Liam, walked quickly over to him. Liam jumped to his feet and held his arms, he could see he was upset. "What's wrong?" He asked; Ashley's eyes filled with water as he blinked them back. Liam walked him to the table. "Nothing now!" Ashley replied; sitting close to his brother. Naz, looked at him, "What animal scared you?" she asked; Ashley lifted his head and looked at her as Liam squeezed his arm and nodded for him to tell them. Ashley looked round the table, 'was Liam actually talking to these girls!'. He looked back at Liam, "Cheetah's" Ashley quietly spoke; 'Cheetah's' the trio said together; Ashley nodded. Liam pat his shoulder "Elephant's" Liam confessed; "Chimps" Naz said; "Lion's" Jemma joined in. Ashley stared at them" you mean you were all frightened of some animal or other!". They all nodded. "What did you do?" Liam asked; Ashley raised his brows, "I ran" he replied; "Actually! I think I was faster than the cheetah's;" Jemma, choked over her coke as they all laughed, Liam, nodding in agreement," He probably was", he laughed. Jemma, looked across at the brothers and saw how happy they were just to be with each other and tears again filled her eyes. Ashley, frowned to Liam. "She is missing her brother" Liam explained; "Oh,

Nathan" Ashley looked at Jemma. "He has just gone in, they won't be long there was only five of them". Jemma cheered up and dried her eyes, she was missing him. The trio sat talking, amazed at how well they were getting on with each other, Jemma glancing at the door every now and then looking for Nathan, 'would they bring him in?'.

Chris Carter, led the fifth group through the doors and stood before the glass door of the chimps. Nathan looked through the door, 'Chimps" he thought. He stood at the door, as the little group went further in, some of the boys tried to go over to them but the chimps moved away. Nathan smiled, 'idiots' he thought. The small group ventured forward leaving Nathan behind, but the chimps moved round them and ended up in the tree near Nathan. Chris Carter, took the group out and went on to the second door, then the third, they reached the fourth door Nathan still wasn't keen on going too far in, but walked a little further just to keep Chris Carter happy. He stopped and had a look round, he couldn't see anything. He watched the other four as they moved further over the grass. Nathan, looked about him, just in front of the fourth door, he noticed a rail which surrounded a huge deep pool. The rail stretched right round the pool breaking off in places to allow entry. Nathan waited for the four to come back then exited the door. Chris Carter looked at Mrs Mason and shook his head. They reached the fifth door as the group went in. Nathan once again staid his distance. He could hear exclamations from the boys and the girl with them lightly screamed. He stared across the field his eyes widening as a hippo walked towards him. Nathan walked slowly back, he had heard that if you run, the hippo would ram you. He took another step, this time quickening his pace, but the hippo walked faster too. Nathan was now panicking. He backed up picking up his speed, as the hippo quickened his. Nathan looked over his shoulder to see how close he was to the door, the sweat, rolling down his face. He Backed out of the door which hadn't closed properly and ran. Unfortunately for Nathan, he ran to quickly and in panic hit the rails and went into the pool. Chris carter, ran to the rail and tried to see if he could see him or if he would have to dive in after him. Nathan surfaced and went back down. He held his breath as he fought to get back up, when something went under him and carried him to the top. Nathan gasped for air and looked down to see who had saved him then fell back when he saw two dolphins at either side of him. Nathan went down again, but this time, something went between his legs and carried him up. Nathan shook the water from his eyes and looked about him. He was sitting on a black and white whale. Panic filled him again and he jumped off its back. He could see steps in the distance and swam towards it, the whale went under and again lifted him up dropping him off at the steps. Nathan grabbed the rail and tried to climb up, but slipped back down, the next he knew, was that one of the dolphins picked him up and placed him on the top step. Nathan gasped for air and backed a little way back on the step. The dolphin swam over to him and put its head on his knee. Nathan stared down at it as it nudged his hand. "Good boy!" Nathan stuttered; Chris Carter, whispered in his ear "He is a she! ". Nathan looked at him. "She wants you to stroke her" He grinned. Nathan looked down at the dolphin and slowly put a gentle finger down the side of her face. The dolphin didn't move. "Good girl" he quietly spoke; The dolphin opened its mouth as if smiling and slowly backed off into the water. Nathan went to stand up, but his legs gave way and he sat down again. Chris Carter grinned, "Let's get you dry". He helped him up and took him over to Barbara Goodall who covered him with a blanket. "Come with me "she said; and led him through the doors to the dining room. Chris Carter looked at Mrs Mason and put five fingers up. Mrs Mason, walked over to him "This hasn't happened in a very long time, let's hope it goes well!". Chris Carter nodded. "Well, you can leave them with us now. If all goes well, we will see you in another five or six years" He smiled; Mrs Mason walked away leaving the five behind.

Nathan, walked through the door, he was dripping wet, but Jemma didn't care. She ran over to him and hugged him tears of relief running down her face. Nathan hugged her back then walked her back to her seat. "You will get soaked "he grinned; He looked round at the others and nodded, "Ok, what's going on?". Every-one caught up with the happenings of the day each telling their story. Nathan sat back in his chair, and frowned. "Why do I feel something isn't right "he said; "and we should have joined the others at the bus for Chippingam by now!" They looked at each other, he was right. Nathan stood up and was about to go to the door, when Barbara Goodall and Chris Carter entered. Barbara Goodall smiled at them. "You all look tired" she spoke; "And you will be wanting to know what is going on. It has been decided that you will stay here with us. It is a lot different from Chippingham, you will be shown to your rooms and will come back here for some tea. Night wear has been provided, you can dress in them for tonight and some-one will bring your clothes later and after you have eaten, we will explain things to you and you can ask questions"; She beckoned for them to follow her and the five got up.

CHAPTER THREE

Barbara Goodall, and Chris Carter, led them through a door which situated a little way to the left as you entered the dining room. The five, followed them along a passage and up some stairs. At the top of the stairs was another long passageway, were doors to rooms stood in line along it. Chris Carter, took the boys to their room, while Barbara Goodall escorted the girls to theirs. This is your room Jemma, you are next to Nathan. All the rooms are the same, so if you want to look round Jemma's room Naz, then you can go straight to your own". Naz nodded, 'she might as well!'. The girls went in. The room was spacious and bright. A double bed was surrounded by fitted wardrobes and besides them, was a on suite. Jemma's eyes lit up "Oh, this is lovely" she smiled; 'and no bars at the window;' at the opposite side of the room, was a patio door. Jemma opened it and found herself standing on a long balcony which stretched from Naz room down to the end room at the other side. Barbara Goodall, walked over, "there is a table and chair for you to sit out, and over here, 'she pointed to a small cupboard' is a coffee machine and kettle. Inside the cupboard, you will find tea bags and coffee, and here is a small fridge just next to the unit where you have cold drinks". Naz and Jemma looked at each other, 'This was wicked'. "Well, I will leave you to settle in, Barbara Goodall spoke; As she turned and walked to the door. "In an hour come down to the dining room and have tea, 'Oh!' Your alarm is set for 9-30am, this is breakfast time and pyjamas and house coat are there on the bed, you may as well be comfy".

Naz went to her room and showered as did the other four. They felt comfortable, and what was even better, was that a TV was fitted up in their room and was discovered on a shelf behind a small wall unit opposite the bed. Naz put on her pyjamas and dressing gown and went out on the balcony. Liam, was already there and nodded to her. Naz looked out of the window the sight of green fields and rolling hills was amazing. "This is beautiful" she spoke across at Liam; "It is rather," he replied; Nathan opened his door, "what is beautiful?" he asked; Liam nodded towards the view, and Nathan went to look just as Jemma joined them. "Have you seen the TV" she asked; They nodded, Nathan glanced across at Liam, "Why do I feel this is all too nice, what are they wanting from us?". Liam frowned," I know just what you mean, this is all too good to be true!". They stood in silence for a while, then Nathan looked at Liam. "Where is your brother?" he asked; just realising he wasn't with them. Liam sighed." He is still doing his hair!" he exclaimed; "No I'm not!" Ashley said; walking out of his door. Liam looked at him, "you have missed a bit" he said; Ashley looked at him and went back in his room only to come straight back out. "I hate you!" he called to Liam. Nathan shook his head and laughed as Liam rolled his eyes, 'what a ham!'. "Well! Are we going for tea, I'm starving!" Ashley complained; Nathan nodded, "Yes we may as well find out exactly what is going on, come on, let's feed you". He said; patting Ashley on the arm, "Food first, info next".

The small group entered the dining room. A kitchen to the right of the room, was now on show, it had been concealed by folding doors but now, the doors were open and one could see the kitchen area. There were trays placed on hot plates and on these were several types of different food. Plates and bowls were stacked at one side and a fridge with ice cream in it looked inviting. "Come on" Nathan said; "It looks like it is Self Service." They helped themselves to the food and ate heartily. "I'm stuffed" Jemma huffed; "Me too!" Naz gasped; The boys sat back in their chairs, 'the food, was good. Twenty minutes later, Barbara Goodall and Chris Carter, entered the room. "Have you all had enough to eat?" Barbara Goodall, asked; They all nodded. "Right! Let's get you all comfortable and we will explain what is going on and why you are here". She led them through another door and into a lounge where comfortable seating was available and the group sat down.

"Where to begin!" Barbara Goodall said; As she sat in a chair, "I guess, at the beginning". She looked across at Chris Carter, then at the door as it opened and a man in a white coat came in. "This is professor Collins". The group nodded as he sat down. Professor Collins, was in his sixties. He was slender in stature, with thick white wavy hair. He wore glasses that looked just a little too big for his face, the black rims resting just above his eyebrows, non-the less, he did look very intelligent. Barbara Goodall, sat back. She sighed and began her story. "In the mid- thirties, German scientist where beginning to experiment on many things. They knew a war was coming and there was hope that they could discover something new to enhance their chances of winning. One such experiment was with animals. Their hope was, that if they could get animals to obey them, they could work with them. These animals would get in places undetected giving them an advantage. Many animals died in their attempt, but dolphins accepted a transmitter which was fastened to their neck and where capable of doing certain things, sadly for the Germans, war came early and although experiments continued, some experiments had to be put aside. One of these experiments was the animal experiment. When America and Brittan walked into Germany, they discovered many document and scientific drawings of experiments that were carried out.

America, took some and so did we, 'We, got the animal experiment'. We too, experimented with the animals in a more human way, and although we had improved on the Germans, we were not making any progress. Then in 1973, a young man 'Bill Gates' created the micro -chip. This opened new doors, as our scientists worked on improving the chip. By the late seventies, the chip had been in planted in several animals, how-ever, the signals were weak and we could only train the animals to do some things. We were no further forward, although if we could succeed, the benefits would be great. By the 1980's we were about to give up, when we were told of a scientist, 'a professor Collins' who had been working on animal behaviour, we quickly grabbed him and welcomed him into our unit. Professor Collins, monitored the animals and a couple of years later, came up with a break through that would change everything. He noticed that animals could talk to each other, but a tiger couldn't talk to a dog. Just like you and I, if we go to France, but can't speak French, then no-one can understand us, or us them, but what if, a way could be found, to transform our words into the sounds of the animal and the animal, into ours, 'a Dr Doolittle effect, Professor Collins, achieved this. Since then we have been working with the animals and it has been a success. Our men and women have been working with them, but even our people retire to start families. This has caused more problems, the animals who worked with the original team, would not work with a new team. Now! We had to remove the chip and we have had to place the animals in zoos and find new ones. This meant we had to train in a new work force every year or two, along with the animals. After a few years of this, it was believed that we may have to look towards a younger work force. But who? We had to be careful who we chose as this is a government project and most of the young people don't have the abilities we need. And then! Out of the blue. One of our staff jokingly said, we should try juveniles. They had plenty of abilities, and what started out as a joke, had promise. If we could be selective, and find the right people this could work.

A plan was made If we operated a correction facility, all the youths who showed promise could go there instead of borstal or prison, and from them, we could choose who was suitable. For the next ten years, all went well, but as the next generation came the animals became selective and wouldn't work with most of them. it was the animals that chose their own work force and only the ones they chose could be used. For the last seventeen years, Mrs Brown has been finding candidates, Mrs Mason has run the correction facility, and myself and crew, this place. But in all that time, the animals have only chosen one or two youths to work with, until now! For the first time in nearly twenty years, the animals have chosen a Five men team." Barbara Goodall, looked at the group, do you want to ask any questions? She asked the group who had sat in silence all the way through her story; Nathan was the first to speak, "what is it that you do here?" he frowned; Barbara Goodall nodded. "Our team works in co-operation with our government, we help retrieve things they need, or rescue those that need rescuing" she replied; Nathan stared back, "you mean, like secret service" he questioned; Barbara Goodall smiled slightly, "just like that" she nodded. The five looked at one another, 'what had they got themselves into!'. "What do we have to do?" Jemma enquired; Her voice sounding concerned. Barbara Goodall looked at her, "You may have to go to places that no-one else can, or retrieve documents that are needed, you may even have to rescue people, but you will do it with the help of the animals, who will do the dangerous things" she consoled her. Professor Collins, smiled. "I will work with you and the animals, so will Chris over there," he said; "Together, we will train you". Barbara Goodall nodded in agreement, "You will also have the freedom to call family, they will be able to come and stay for a week, every now and then and we will provide a cottage so you can stay with them. You are free to walk in the grounds and we will go on trips at times, but what you can't do, is tell them what you do, they have to go on thinking you are still in a more relaxed correction facility". Chris Carter, stood up, "you are not prisoners anymore, you are part of a team and will do important things, your training will start tomorrow".

The next day, the five came down for breakfast, they had been talking thing's through most of the night and were still feeling tired. Chris Carter, came through the door and glanced at them." Oh dear!" He exclaimed; "I guess you didn't get much sleep then". Jemma yawned "not really" she replied; Chris Carter shook his head, I guess we will have to give you a couple of hours to wake up, then we start". By 11am, the group had been taken to the chimp area. "We are going to get you use to the animals this week, so let's start by introducing you to the chimps" Professor Collins announced; The five spent the week getting over their fear, they were amazed at how compliant the animals were, and how well they obeyed the commands given to them. The week-end came around, Jemma and Naz, spent their time doing their hair and nails, while the boys took themselves to the garden. They had all phoned their parents, who were relieved to hear them sounding more content and settled. By Monday the five were ready to start work with the animals. Ashley thought it was rather cool to be able to talk to the animals, whilst Nathan and Liam were interested in how to control them. Jemma and Naz were not that interested, although they did like the chimps.

Chris Carter escorted the five to the chimp area. They had been given a chain necklace which hung round their neck like a choker and which had a centre piece of an ornamental circle of leaves and in the centre of this, was what looked like a grey stone, but in fact, was the microchip which gave out the signals of command and altered the tones to suite each animal. "The first thing you need to learn, is that when you give a command to the animals, you must say which animal you are giving the command to" He explained; "If you give it to a lion, you must say lion, to a chimp, chimp, dolphin, dolphin, do you understand!" he asked; They all nodded. "Got it" said Nathan. "Right Naz, do you want to try?". Naz looked at him, she was unsure, but nodded "Ok!" she replied; and walked over to where the chimps were sitting. "Say chimp" Chris Carter told her. Naz looked at a chimp, 'Chimp,' she said; The chimp looked up, "Now tell him to go to the top of the tree", coached Carter. "Naz looked at the chimp "Go to the top of the tree" she commanded; The chimp looked putting his head to one side to let her know he was listening. "Go to the top," she pointed at Jemma's tea shirt which had a tree printed on it," the top of the tree," she pointed to the tree. The chimp sprang into action, it pulled Jemma's top over her head and took it to the top of the tree. Jemma screamed and ran behind the tree her tea shirt was in. Naz, was horrified, but the boys, including Chris Carter, cried with laughter. "Carter gave an order to the chimp and he brought the top down, "here" he called to Jemma, and handed her the tea shirt. Jemma came out from behind the tree. "that wasn't funny" she said indignantly. Naz cringed, "sorry" she spoke," I didn't mean too!". The elephants were the next to be visited. Liam, was not to happy, he remembered the last time he saw them. "Nathan," Carter called; "Give the elephant an order. Nathan gaped at him, "what do you want me to say "he asked, confused. "Something simple" replied Carter; Liam backed away, he was too close to Nathan, if anything went wrong he didn't want to be in the firing line. Nathan sighed, "ok here goes. Elephant," he said; sounding in total control. Liam backed further away, Nathan looked at him and gestured his arm to indicate for him to come closer, "elephant the branch." He pointed up at the tree. The elephant instantly obeyed. It lifted his trunk and picking up Liam, sat him in the tree. Every-one stared, open mouthed. Chris Carter closed his eyes and shook his head. He turned to the elephant, but before he could give an order, Liam shouted down. "No!" he exclaimed; "Move the elephant and I will get down myself". The elephant moved and Liam jumped from the tree giving Nathan an angry glare. Nathan squinted his eyes. Chris Carter sighed, "come on" let's try something else". The group visited several animals and ended up in the lion's area. The lions came over to them and were given strokes. "Jemma, put her hand up," Can I give them an order?" she asked; Carter nodded," be my guest". Jemma stood back a little and moved Naz with the back of her hand placing her behind herself. "Lion, sit" she commanded. The lion looked at her and in a flash, had knocked Naz to the ground and sat on her. Naz gasped, "get it off me" she groaned; Chris Carter, rolled his eyes and gave the order for the lion to move. "Did you do that on purpose!" she complained; turning to Jemma. "No!" Jemma snorted back. Carter jumped in quick. "Let's try one or two more, then let's call it a day". The Cheetah's and Dolphins were next, but disaster struck in each case. Ashley ended up being chased into a cave and slavered over, ruining his hair. Nathan, was lifted on the tail of the wale, and ended up being flung over the rail which surrounded the pool. Chris carter, called it a day, as the five hobbled their way back to their rooms. Jemma tugging at her top, Naz holding her stomach. Liam, limping, Ashley, fighting with his hair which was standing up on his head and Nathan, holding his back. All looking such a sorrowful sight. Barbara Goodall, walked over to Chris carter, "how is it going?" she asked; Carter shook his head, "not good" he replied; "Still, it's early days".

Several weeks passed and the five were still struggling. "What do you think Chris?" Barbara Goodall asked; "They are not ready" he replied; "I'm beginning to think they will never be, they are great kids not like the usual juvenile, but their hearts are not in it". Barbara Goodall sighed, "their parents are coming up for a week, let's see how they are after they go" Chris carter nodded, personally, he thought it would make them worse, but who was he to say so. Nathan, Jemma, Liam, Ashly and Naz. Couldn't wait to see their parents it had seemed like years since they had seen them. The full week had been bliss, but as it came to an end Jemma once again was in tears. Her mum hugged and kissed her, and told her how proud she was of her for sticking it out. Jemma was still in tears as the mini bus that was taking the parents to the train station, pulled away. Nathan, hugged her," Come on he gently spoke; Ashley too, was upset by his mother's departure and if he could have gotten away with it, would have been in the bus with her. Liam gently squeezed his arm," you know we can't, don't worry bro, I'm not going to leave you, we will do this together". Ashley sadly nodded, but he had never been so glad to have his brother with him. Naz walked towards them still in tears, the four looked at her, Naz didn't have a brother or sister and was totally alone, but not any longer, they were in this together and she was now part of them, they all crowded round her and gave her a hug. Naz smiled through wet eyes and looked round at them all as they made their way to the car that would take them back to Hillock, for the first time, she felt she belonged.

Two weeks had gone by since their parents had gone home and the five had settled back down to working with the animals. They had finally bonded with them, but struggled giving them commands. Chris Carter, was almost ready to give up and had said as such to professor Collins. "I think we are going to have to speak with Barbara "Professor Collins turned to Chris Carter, "This is very disappointing!". As the men were talking, Barbara Goodall, popped her head out of her office and beckoned to the men to come. "We have an assignment, are they ready?". She asked; Professor Collins and Chris Carter, looked at each other, Professor Collins sighed," they have all the abilities, but for some reason, they are not using them". Barbara Goodall, glanced at them, "It's too late, we need them now! Bring them to the lounge to be briefed, and get them ready".

The five were brought to the lounge and were given drinks. Barbara Goodall looked at them. "An assignment has come in and we need your help". The five looked round at every-one, 'were they ready? They didn't feel ready'. "Chris will be with you all the way" she continued; "The assignment is this. An American ambassador visited our prime minister at Downing Street. With him was an important document that had to be signed. The document was signed and placed in the brief case that the ambassador brought with him and was chained to his wrist. The ambassador and his body guards, were escorted to their jet and the plane took off landing hours later in Washington. The steps to the plane were lowered, but no-one got off. One of the pilots went to investigate and found the ambassador and his body guard's dead and the briefcase which contained the document, now contained a roll of newspaper. It is believed that some form of gas was placed in the air system of the plane which killed all on board except for the pilots who were in a different room. The Americans, believe the Russians are involved, but hold us responsible, it's our job to get the document back".

Nathan looked concerned. "How are we going to do that" he asked; Barbara Goodall looked at him, "One of our spies found out that a Russian spy had landed at Gatwick just an hour before the Ambassadors plane. It is possible he joined the bodyguards at some point or managed to get in to Downing street, either way, the Russian spy was caught and given a truth serum, under its influence, he spoke of a yacht which belonged to a Turkish millionaire. The yacht is harboured in Barcelona, then will make its way to Turkey. we believe the document is on board. It is believed it was passed on, some-one on that yacht has it, if it falls in the hands of the Russians, it could ruin diplomatic relations. We have to find it and get it back in safe hands, your task, is to do that" Liam frowned, "how will we do that?" he asked; Barbara Goodall looked across at Carter. "You don't!" she replied; "The girls do". Nathan shook his head, "I'm not letting our Jemma, or Naz, go alone" he complained; "It could be dangerous. Barbara Goodall looked firmly at him, "Boris Lavinski, is a multimillionaire his birth home is Bosnia, but spends most of his time sailing round in his yacht. He throws parties, but only invites the wealthy, but he has a liking for young pretty girls. If Jemma and Naz can get on board his yacht, they may be able to scout round and discover who may have the document or even retrieve it". Nathan was still not happy. Liam and Ashley were not convinced either. Barbara Goodall, sighed; "We would normally use the animals, but you haven't got the hang of using them yet and we can't put them in danger". There was still a look of discontent in the boys faces. Chris Carter, leaned over to Barbara Goodall and whispered in her ear. There was silence for a few seconds, then she turned to the boys, "What if we arranged for you to stay on board our own yacht, but you will have to stay far back". The boys looked at each other, then nodded,' at least they would be nearby. "You will all be equipped with a communication necklaces, Jemma, Naz, you will have a mike in your purse so you can talk to us, please say 'humans' first as the necklace will also pick up your conversation and the animals will think it is for them. You will all be issued a passport, and a Euro visa card. These, you will carry with you at all times." She turned to the girls, "When you dock in Turkey, you will leave the yacht and make your way to different hotels where you can buy new clothes to change into. From there you will go to different airports. Jemma, you will fly to Manchester, where you will be picked up. Naz, you will fly to Spain and from there to Tees-side. You boys will be brought back by yacht, but if things go wrong! You will make your way to the nearest train, plane and ship, and make your way to Teesside airport where you will be picked up, Jemma once at Manchester, get a taxi to Teesside, that will be the meeting point. Lavinski's yacht docks in three hours, we will fly you girls out and you can be in the casino by tonight, Lavinski will be there. Evening wear will be given to you on the plane, now go and get ready".

CHAPTER FOUR

Three hours later, the girls arrived at the hotel. They had been given a bag each which contained their evening dress and made their way to their rooms. That evening Jemma and Naz got dressed and headed for the casino. As they entered, heads turned. The girls did look stunning. Jemma's Black hair complimented the long light blue evening gown which was edged with silver braiding. One strap clung to her right shoulder, leaving the left shoulder bare. Her silver shoes, co-ordinating with her dress and diamond earrings, Jemma looked beautiful. Naz, too, looked amazing. Her black hair was pinned up on top of her head were a red thick band with gold braid surrounded it. Her deep red strapless long dress showed off her slender figure, and her smooth slender black shoulders, her red shoes also co-ordinated with her dress as did her gold earrings with rubies in it. Naz looked like a film star. The girls walked in and it wasn't long before they were approached. Naz lifted her purse to her face, "we are in" she whispered; "We will keep you informed".

Nathan, Liam, and Ashley. Made their way in the yacht several miles to where Lavinski had moored. Ashley fiddled with his hair as the sea air had taken the gel out of it. The boys rolled their eyes, 'Ashley was such a wimp'. An hour or so had gone by and the boys were getting restless. Chris Carter brought them a drink and a light meal, "We should hear something soon" he told them. Jemma and Naz, were still in the casino, their host had certainly noticed them as he had both on each of his arms. The girls walked with him and stood with him at the roulette table till 1-30am. Lavinsky waved to one of his men and turned to the girls "Come, my darlings, we go to my yacht". Naz and Jemma, smiled and nodded. Jemma held his attention while Naz, spoke quietly into her purse. "Humans, we are heading for the yacht". The girls boarded the yacht and glanced round, several people had been invited and the yacht looked quite full. "Where do we start!" Naz exclaimed; Glancing at Jemma. "Let's split up, you take the left side and I will go right, we will meet back here in an hour" she replied; The girls split up and started to look round the yacht. Most of the females wore tight dresses, nothing could be hidden in there, and they, like Naz and Jemma, had been picked up from the casino. The men wore evening suits which lay flat and un creased, one would see if anything was bulging the pockets. Both girls met back were they had started as the yacht set off to sea. "Let's check the staff" Naz turned to Jemma. Jemma nodded back. The girls walked the deck inspecting each of the working staff but found nothing. They stood near the rail looking out at sea, 'what else could they do!' Jemma lifted her purse, "we have found nothing" she spoke; "Perhaps that's because you may be looking in the wrong place" a voice behind them spoke. The girls turned, to see a pretty woman in her mid-twenties, her long blond hair pulled back off her face with diamond studded combs. "I have been watching you, can I ask what you are looking for!" she asked; Jemma and Naz glanced at each other, "what makes you think we are looking for something" Jemma replied; "And why have you been watching us," Naz enquired. The woman, lifted her shawl which was draped over her arm and hand, and produced a small pistol. "Let's go down to the cabin area, we can talk better there". The girls stiffened, but obeyed, 'there was nothing else they could do'. "where is the document?" the woman asked; "What document!" Jemma bluffed; "Don't!" the woman responded; Jemma was silent. 'Drop the gun' a deep voice spoke and the click of gun was heard. The woman dropped the gun and walking towards the girls turned. A man in his forties was holding a revolver which had a silencer on it, and was pointing it at them. "Walk down to the cabin at the end" he ordered;

Slightly moving the gun in the direction of the cabin. The three did as they were told and opening the cabin door, was forced inside.

"Who are you working for" he asked; Silence filled the air. "I won't ask again" he threatened; His finger moved on the trigger, but noises from outside, stopped him. "You" he turned to the woman with the blond hair, "Tie them up". He threw some cord at her and she began tying Jemma, and Naz hands and feet. "Now you, get on the bed and put your hands behind your back" he ordered; The woman did as she was told and was tied up too. Jemma stared at him, "what do you want?" she asked; The man swept back his dark hair which had streaks of grey in it and which strands of it fell over his eyes. A scar lined his forehead and his eyes were dark and a little slanted. "The document!" The woman answered for him. The man walked over to Jemma and placed a pillow case which he used as a gag in her mouth, but as he did so, his white coat which he had put on, insinuating he was part of the staff, fell open and Jemma caught a glance of a roll of paper in his breast pocket. He finished gagging them and leaving the room, locked the door behind him. The woman, rolled off the bed and on to her knees, then on her knees, made her way to where Naz lay on the floor. Naz eyes widened, as the woman came close to her mouth, then pulling the gag with her teeth, freed it, then Jemma. "Who are you?" Jemma asked; As she freed the woman from her gag. The woman smiled, "my name is Sam Sanders, I work for M.I.5. And you!". Jemma looked at Naz. "We too, work for a secret organisation and are after the document, for Brittan's sake." She explained; "Probably to give it to M.I.5." Naz joined in. "Well neither of us is going to get it if we can't get out of here" Sam complained; "Can't we unlock the door, you know like using a hair pin?" Naz enquired; as Sam fidgeted with her cord to free her, making her fingers swollen and saw as they sat back to back while Sam untied the knot. "Yes" she replied; "But he has probably left the key in the lock, if so, it won't work." Sam Sanders, looked about her, she was an attractive woman her light blue eyes were large and fetching and she had that gentleness about her, although she had proven she could be tough if she needed to be.

"There is no way out of here" she exclaimed; But Jemma was already looking at the porthole. "If I can get through that porthole, I could climb up to the rail and get on deck. I could then come and unlock the door and free you both." Sam Sanders frowned; "It's impossible, isn't it?"; Naz grinned, and looked across at Jemma. "Not for her" she nodded towards Jemma. Jemma went to the porthole and opened it, she could see the deck rail, it wasn't that far up if she could get on the porthole and stand on its rim, she could reach the rail easy. She looked round the room and picked up a sheet from the bed. "Tie this round my waist" she asked Naz; Naz did as she was asked and tied the sheet round her waist. "Now hold on to the other end and support me both of you". Jemma climbed on to the porthole with one leg out, the other hanging down the wall in the room. She had tied her dress up round her waist with the help of a pillowcase and carried her purse in her mouth. 'Easy" she thought to herself. She gripped the top of the porthole and swung her other leg out. Naz and Sam, gripped the end of the sheet taking the strain of Jemma's weight. Jemma gripped the top of the porthole and carefully stood up, she reached out one hand and gripped the rail which surrounded the deck, then letting go, grabbed the rail with her second hand. Jemma dangled down the side of the yacht, then pushing herself up, climbed over the rail and onto the deck. She undid the sheet round her waist and lowered her dress. "Told you she could" Naz grinned at Sam. Jemma made her way across the deck towards the cabin area but half way there she saw the waiter who had imprisoned them. He was talking to a waitress and was in deep conversation. Jemma watched on, but to her horror, saw him hand her something, 'oh no!" she exclaimed; The waiter had handed her the document from under his coat," there are two of them" Jemma sighed. She was about to move when the waitress walked over in her direction and passing her, walked towards the cabin area. Jemma followed picking up a rolled napkin as she went. The waitress stopped at a cupboard just at the entrance and placing the document on a small table unlocked the cupboard door. Crouching down, Jemma stretched out her arm and swapped over the rolls. The door to the cupboard had blocked the waitress eyes from seeing what Jemma had done and taking out a towel, quickly covered the scroll with it and placed it at the back of the cupboard.

Jemma watched as the waitress moved away placing the key in her pocket. She hurried down to the cabin and unlocking the door, released the girls. "We will have to keep a low profile till we dock" Sam Sander's whispered; "And we have to find the document". Jemma looked at Naz and smiled, "Not necessarily" she replied; taking the scroll from the bust of her dress. Sam and Naz looked aghast, "you have the document, but how?" Sam enquired; "I will tell you later" Jemma replied; "Let's just get away from here". They made their way to the deck, their only hope was that they were not spotted. The girls mingled with the other guests talking and laughing and every now and then walked on to some-one new. They would reach Turkey in one hour, then they could slip ashore and make their way back to Spain and home.

Sam Sanders, was irritable. She just wanted to get off the yacht. She stood talking to other guests with her back turned away from the deck and looked out to sea. 'Oh, thank you' said a member of the little group Sam was standing with, as they took a glass of wine from a tray the waiter had brought. Sam turned to take a glass and stared in the face of the waiter who hunted them. His eyes narrowed as he looked in surprise at her wondering how she had escaped. Sam bowed her head to the guests and making her excuse, backed away towards Naz and Jemma. "We have been compromised" she quietly spoke; The girls looked across at the waiter who had now been joined by his partner. "What are we going to do?" Jemma asked; "I don't know" Sam frowned; "We are trapped on the yacht, and there is no way we can get off. "They looked round hoping to find a way out, but with no avail. "Human" Naz spoke; "We are trapped, we Have the document but can't get off the yacht, there are two spies, not one and they are both after us, we need help".

Chris Carter, sat on deck He had been waiting to hear from the girls and patiently read his paper. Nathan, Liam, and Ashley, looked out to sea. Nathan was worried, he hadn't heard from Jemma since she went aboard the yacht. The sun was beginning to rise, the girls had been gone all night. Nathan looked at Chris Carter and walked over to where he sat, "Why haven't we heard from the girls?" he asked; Chris Carter, scratched his head, and yawned. "Maybe, it's because things are going well and they are waiting till they get to Turkey" he replied; Nathan sighed and walked back to where the boys sat. He still wasn't happy. The sky was getting brighter and the sun was beginning to rise in the heavens. Chris Carter stood up and walked towards the boys. "The girls will reach Turkey in an hour" he informed them patting Nathan on the shoulder. Nathan looked at him, he wouldn't be happy until Jemma was safely back with him. Liam and Ashley leaned over the rail, "do you think they are alright?" Ashley whispered to Liam. "I don't know, I think it's a bit strange that if they are almost there, that they haven't contacted us saying so" he whispered back. "I'm beginning to think the same thing" Nathan joined in, as he leaned over the rail too. Ashley looked blankly out to sea. What are you thinking?" Liam asked him. He knew his brother, when Ashley went blank, it was because something was on his mind. Ashley blinked, "I'm thinking we have to do something, but I don't know what!". Nathan looked at Liam, "He's right, something just doesn't feel right" he agreed. Chris Carter, looked towards the boys, "It will be!" he was about to say over soon, when Naz voice anxiously came over the microphone." We need help!". The boys jumped from the rail listening intently to what she was saying. Chris Carter, jumped to attention and shouted an order to one of the crew members, "Get me Hillock on the phone, I think we are going to have to follow the yacht into Turkey, tell them we may need back up. Nathan, paced the deck, 'this was not good! This was definitely not good'. Barbara Goodall, spoke to Carter. "Stay where you are," she told him. "If you go in, innocent people could get hurt, not to mention the document could get passed on. I will notify the Turkish police saying we believe the yacht is a cover for drug smuggling, leave it to them".

Carter glanced at the boys," It's under control" he called to them; Nathan didn't believe him. By the time help reached the girls, they could be hurt or even worse. "We have got to do something!" he turned to the boys. "We know, but what?", Liam asked; "We can always call the animals" Ashley said; Resting his chin on his hands as he leaned on the rail. "Yes," Liam groaned," And we will probably end up in China".

Nathan, thought for a few minutes, "Not necessarily" he exclaimed; "Remember, we just have to give them basic orders and say the name of the animal so they know who we are talking to". The boys looked at him, "But it will take hours for them to reach us" Ashley spoke. Nathan sighed, he was probably right. "No!" Liam turned to them, "It's been known for dolphins to travel miles in a short space of time, if we call them now, they could reach us in maybe an hour ". They looked at each other, "Let's do it" Nathan quietly spoke, I have a plan". He lifted the necklace round his neck and spoke into it. "Dolphins, follow the signal and come to the yacht. Whale, follow the Dolphins". He looked at Liam and Ashley, "We need to get by the crew and activate the signal for the Dolphins to follow". Ashley, took a step forward, "Create a disturbance, and leave the rest to me" he smiled. Nathan and Liam found some papers and rolled them into a ball and started to play a game of football. The crew joined in, every now and then, kicking the paper back to them, while Ashley sneaked his way to where the switch was to send the signal.

Nathan and Liam played football till the roll of paper ended up going over board and into the ocean. Nathan looked round to see if Ashley was ok, only to find Ashley leaning on the rail and smiling. "How does he do that?" Nathan exclaimed; Liam shook his head "Don't ask" he grinned. The boys leaned back on the rail as Nathan explained what his plan was. "Do you understand?" he asked; "What if we can't get the document" Liam queried. "Naz said there were two spies, once I'm on board, she can point them out to me. I will get the girls off the yacht and look for the document myself, as soon as I have found it I will pass it to you Ashley, you will then tell the dolphin to take you to shore, and get back to England. You have your wallet with the Euro money card, use it. Liam, you will help the girls, get them on the dolphin and tell the dolphin to head for the shore, then you and I will go back on the whale. "The boys nodded, the plan seemed sound.

Chris Carter, was busy talking to the crew. He looked calm, but his body actions indicated he was worried. He had no idea what the boys were up to, if he had, he would have stopped them. Nathan, Liam and Ashley, kept watch, 'how long would it take the dolphins to arrive'. The boys were given coke to drink and drank it still leaning over the side of the yacht. Ashley, stood at the rail while Nathan and Liam went to sit down. He gazed out to sea, the ocean was calm. He sighed as he looked to his right, in the distance, he thought he saw a large wave. He strained his eyes. 'There it goes again' he thought to himself. He continued to stare when he saw a huge tail come right out of the water. Nathan, Liam, he whispered. "They are coming, they are coming". Nathan and Liam, went to the rail as the dolphins also came to the surface, "YES!" Nathan grinned, "right, you both know what you have to do". The boys nodded and looked round to see what Carter and the crew were doing, then the three, slipped over the side and gripped on to the rail. As the dolphins came close to the yacht, they slipped into the water and clung on to the dolphin's fin. Nathan was the stronger swimmer and swam further out till he reached the whale and climbed onto it's back. Liam bent his head and spoke into his necklace. "Swim ahead" he commanded. The dolphin didn't need to be told twice, it took off at a good speed. Ashley did the same and in no time at all, was side by side with Liam. Nathan sat on the wales back and leaning forward, gripping to its fin, gave his command, "Whale, follow the dolphins". The whale moved forward, then with his tail moving from side to side, picked up speed and in only a few minutes, had caught up with the dolphins.

Barbara Goodall, was about to make a phone call to the Turkish police. She picked up the phone and dialled the number, when Professor Collins burst through her door, "come quick he called to her, "I think you will want to see this". Barbara Goodall put down the phone a puzzled expression on her face and followed him to the dolphin arena. "Look!" he exclaimed; And pointed to the dolphins and whale. Barbara Goodall stared as the dolphins and whale, went frantically round and round. She looked across at professor Collins, "how long have they been doing this?" she asked; He shrugged his shoulders, "I am not sure" he replied; The dolphins had to travel down a long tunnel before they reached the sea, this tunnel had a huge metal gate which had to be raised to let them free. Barbara Goodall watched on for a few minutes then as the dolphins and wale grew more frantic, she gave the order, "OPEN THE GATE!". One of the female assistants pressed the red button which opened the gate and the dolphins and whale sped through. Professor Collins monitored their course, "They are heading far out to sea" he told Barbara Goodall. "But what their destination is, I don't know!". Barbara Goodall, picked up her phone "Chris" she spoke; "The dolphins are free, have you called them?" Chris Carter, frowned," no, do you know where they are going?" Barbara Goodall sighed; "Not yet, has the boys called them?" Chris Carter looked across at the boys, "I don't think so, they are playing football with the crew, I wonder if the girls have." Barbara Goodall, frowned, "Chris, someone has, keep an eye on the sea, they are going somewhere, I will ring you later". Carter tried to stay calm, but with the worry of the girls and now the dolphins, he was a little uneasy. Almost an hour went by, Carter had watched the ocean intently, but with no luck. The boys were now drinking coke and leaning on the rail, it didn't look like they were going anywhere. He went to get a drink when his phone went off. "Have you seen anything yet?" Barbara Goodall, spoke; Carter, sighed, "no not a thing, the boys!". Carter stopped and hastily walked the deck. "Where are the boys?" he asked the rest of the crew. Every-one glanced round the deck, but the boys had gone. "The boys have gone" he told Barbara Goodall, "there is no sign of them or the dolphins and whale". Barbara Goodall went silent, she remembered what Carter had said about the five working with the animals and slightly smiled, "useless eh Chris, let me know if you hear or see anything" and she put the phone down.

The dolphins neared the yacht the girls were on. "Dolphins stop" Nathan commanded. The dolphins instantly stopped bringing the whale to a stop too. Liam and Ashley climbed off their backs and swam to Nathan and boarded the whale. "Dolphins swim to the side of the yacht" Nathan gave the order and pointed to the side of the yacht that was furthest away from them. He then commanded the whale to swim near the yacht, the whale did what was asked of it. The boys were close to the side of the yacht, while the dolphins, 'at the other side', entertained the guests on the yacht who had seen them and had moved to the side to watch them. Nathan moved to the whale's tail, "Whale, lift your tail". The whale lifted its tail till Nathan was the same Hight of the rail. Nathan looked around the deck, Jemma and Naz were standing near the rail with another female, and in front of them was the spy and his accomplice a small pistol in his hand covered by a white towel preventing any-one seeing it except the girls. Nathan weighed up the situation then bending down a little, spoke into his necklace. "Whale spout water onto the deck". For a few seconds the wale did nothing, then a fountain of water gushed from it, drenching the deck. The assassins, dropped their guard giving Nathan a chance to jump over the rail and punch the waiter on the jaw. The gun fell from his hand and Nathan picked it up. He pointed the gun towards the cabin area, indicating for them to walk that way, and once inside the cabin, 'with Jemma's help, tied them up.

Jemma, turned and looking at Nathan, wrapped her arms around his neck and held on. Nathan hugged her back, he was just glad she was safe and sound. Naz walked forward, "It's good to see you" she said; Nathan smiled and gave her a hug too, 'he liked Naz'. "Come on" he said; Let's get out of here, but first, we have to find the document, do you know where they put it?". Jemma smiled and putting her hand down the front of her dress, pulled the document out. Nathan, grinned and shook his head, 'that was his Jemma'. He took the document from her and led them to the rail. "Ashley" he called; Ashley looked up as Nathan threw the document to him, "you know what to do, now go and do it". Ashley lowered his head, "Dolphin, take me to the shore". The dolphin sped off leaving its partner and whale behind. Naz and Jemma, stared at the animals. "Your handling the animals!" Jemma exclaimed; Nathan grinned, "for now, let's hope things go well". Naz waved at Liam, he was still sitting on the whale, 'it was good to see them all'. "Right" Nathan called; "Let's get you off this yacht". He held Jemma by the arm but Jemma pulled back." Wait!" she exclaimed; "Sam, has to come too". Nathan, looked across at the young woman standing by Naz side. "This is Sam Sanders, she's M.I.5 and was also looking for the document" Nathan rubbed his hands over his chin, he hadn't counted on a third party. He looked down at Liam "We have a problem, we have to take one more" Liam looked up at Sam Sanders "ok", she will have to go on the other dolphin though" He replied; Nathan nodded and explained what she had to do, "help her down" he called to Liam. Liam helped her over to the dolphin and she grabbed hold of its fin. Liam gave it, its order. "Take her to the shore line". The dolphin sped off as Sam Sanders gave a light scream.

Ashley reached the shore. The dolphin stopped a little way out so as not to get trapped in shallow water. Ashley had wrapped the document in a plastic cover and slipping off the dolphin placed it in his mouth and swam, butterfly style to the shore. He sat on the beach, a little out of breath, then told the dolphin who was waiting for an order, to go back to the whale. The dolphin swam backwards a little, then turning swam off. Ashley walked up the beach, he was drenched, but as the sun shone down, his clothes began to dry, steaming as they did so. He walked up some steps to a market place, he needed to buy some dry clothes, it wasn't likely they would take his plastic card, he needed a bank. He walked further on leaving the market place behind and ended up in a large shopping mall which was surrounded by high rise buildings. 'I must be in a large town or city' Ashley thought to himself, 'I wonder where!'. He walked through the mall, his clothes were dry but his wet shoes squeaked. he found a bank Konyaalıtı bank 'so, I must have come ashore on Konyaalit Beach. He thought. He drew out a couple of hundred pounds in Euro's and went and bought new clothes. He bought food and then made his way to the airport. He looked at the flight board, there was a plane leaving in two hours for Manchester, he was going to be on it. He went to get his ticket and sat in the waiting area. People were coming in, mostly families. Ashley went to get a coffee and sat back down, he suddenly felt home sick. He sipped at his coffee and thought. 'What if he got a taxi from Manchester to Hartlepool, he could be home in five hours and be with his mam. Liam would know what he would do, and might do the same'. For a few minutes, he felt happy, then doubt crept in. 'What if Liam didn't, he would be left alone at Hillock'. Ashley battled with his conscience as his boarding flight come over the loud speaker and wrapping the document up in a magazine he had bought, made his way to the passage which would take him to his plane. Ashley lingered, letting other people go first, his mind in tatters 'should he, shouldn't he?'

Sam Sanders, fought her way to the shore, she was not a strong swimmer, and was delighted to reach the stone beach. She sat for a few minutes drying off, she looked round the shore line, 'where was the first boy! He was nowhere in sight'. She walked along the beach, the pebbles hurting her feet. 'It seemed to her, that the beach stretched for miles'. Finally, she reached some stone steps and climbed them, finding herself, in a small market. She headed for a phone, and dialled a code number and in twenty minutes, Sam Sanders was flown home.

The first dolphin came back to the yacht, "Naz it's your turn" Nathan called; Naz climbed on its back and gave the command. The dolphin headed for the shore. Naz, was also a poor swimmer, and spluttered her way towards the golden sandy beach. She lay on the beach gasping for air," Thank you god, thank you!" she spoke out loud. She sat up and looked about her, Sam Sanders and Ashley, were nowhere in sight. She could see large buildings in the near distance and made her way towards them. "Where am I?" she wondered; She walked to the town and headed towards a nearby bank. 'Konyaalit' she read.' I wonder if that's the name of the town' she said to herself. She walked into the bank and cashed some Euro's and headed for the nearest airport. She looked at the flight board, but there were no flights to England till the early hours of the following morning. 'Damn! she thought. She checked the flight board again, and discovered a flight to France. 'Well, she thought, if I catch that flight, I could get a flight to England from there, or get a train, go through the tunnel, and get a flight in London to Tees-side'. She obtained her ticket and sat in the waiting area, people were coming in and going out from all over the world. She looked round at the families and how happy they were and the thought of seeing Dad, flooded her mind. If she got to London, she had family there, she could get lost in London and no-body would be able to find her, Dad could visit. She sat and thought. Dad would not be happy if police were knocking at his door, and he would have to give names and addresses of family in London too. She sighed, surely Dad would let her stay till they could think of something. She was deep in thought when her flight came over the loud speaker, she boarded the plane, her mind racing. The plane finally landed and Naz walked out on French soil. She walked over to the flight board and discovered a flight that would take her to London. She bought something to eat and drink while she waited for her flight and pondered over what she should do. 'Flights to London are now boarding' came the voice over the speaker, Naz stood up and stared down the corridor that would take her to her plane, she had made good friends at Hillock, they had her back, but she also wanted to see her dad, 'What was she going to do?'.

The second dolphin had now returned and Liam slipped off the whale and on to the dolphin. "Are you coming?" he turned to Nathan. Nathan nodded," I just want to get Jemma safe first" he replied; Liam nodded back, "then I will wait with you, let Jemma take this dolphin and I will get the second". Nathan, smiled. He knew Liam wanted to get to Ashley yet he was willing to stay back to keep Jemma safe, that showed character, he admired that. Just as Jemma was climbing over the side, the first dolphin returned, "never mind" Nathan called to Liam, you go, I will get Jemma on the other dolphin. Liam nodded and gave the order to the dolphin. Minutes later, Liam found himself on the same part of the beach Ashley had landed on. Liam stood up and headed for the market place. He found the bank in the town and made his way to the airport. Liam looked on the flight board, but there were no flights that day, 'what was he going to do now!'. He stood around looking lost then noticed one of the airport attendants, he went over to him and explained he needed to get to England that day and was there somewhere he could get a flight. The attendant thought for a few moments, then nodded. 'You can get a taxi to Istanbul, they may have a flight there'. Liam thanked him and jumped into a taxi. A few hours later Liam arrived at Istanbul airport and made his way to the flight board 'Yes! There was a flight to Gatwick' He booked his flight and sat back and waited to board. He wondered were Ashley was, 'oh no!' he thought. 'surely he wouldn't head for home'. He frowned, then sighed, 'yes! He would'. Now he had a problem, did he go home, or had he gone back to Hillock. Liam thought long and hard, maybe if he went home he could see if he was there first, but then, how could he just turn up at Hillock days or weeks later, if Ashley hadn't gone home, it would mean he would have left him on his own at Hillock and worse, they could split them up. Liam was lost and didn't know what to do for the best. 'Flights to Gatwick, now boarding,' the voice over the speaker was heard. Liam stood up but couldn't move, 'what was he going to do?'.

Nathan, called to Jemma, "come on" he said; "Let's get you home". Jemma climbed over the side and onto the dolphins back, "Go to the shore" Jemma commanded, and the dolphin obeyed. In a few moments, Jemma was on the shore, "go back to the whale" she told the dolphin as it turned and headed back. Jemma walked to the town she had no idea where she was or how she was going to get home. She made it to the airport but soon discovered there was no flights that day. Jemma looked lost and it didn't take long for a woman to ask if she was alright. Jemma explained her plight as the woman carefully listened. "You could get a boat to Konya, it will take several hours, but you can get a flight from there". Jemma thanked the woman and was thankful she spoke English. She made her way to the docks and asked if anybody spoke English and was surprised to find many people did. She looked round for some-one she could trust to take her to Konya and thankfully found an old man and his son who were willing to do it. Almost four hours later, Jemma arrived at Konya. She made her way to the airport and was thankful to find a flight was due in two hours. Jemma collected her ticket and sat in the waiting room, she was just happy to be going home, she couldn't wait to see Nathan safe and sound too. She got herself a drink and looked out of the window it was getting dark. She began to wonder where Nathan was, and a terrible thought struck her,' what if he went home, he would think she would do that, should she go home? But if she did, would Nathan be there, she couldn't leave him alone at Hillock, what should she do!'.

Nathan stood on the deck of the yacht. He had become aware that he had been noticed by Lavinski who was already asking his guests who he was. Nathan looked round, coming from the cabin area, was the waiter and his assistant who had somehow got free. He was in danger and he knew it. He backed towards the rail and dived into the ocean, as he sank further down, a large figure settled under his body and carried him back to the surface. Nathan coughed and spluttered, then gaining his repose, called out to the whale, "Whale swim out to see". The whale took off leaving the yacht far behind, the dolphins following close by. After what seemed a long time, Nathan commanded the whale to swim to shore. The whale turned and headed in land, far in the distance Nathan could see land and as the whale came closer, he told the whale to stop, while he changed from the whale to the dolphin. Nathan gripped the fin of the dolphin," swim to shore" he commanded. The dolphin swam closer to the shore line, then slipping off it, he swam to the shore. Nathan found himself on a beach, mixed with pebbles and sand and wondered where he was. He knew he had been in the water for some time as his hands had pruned. He had also noticed the change of temperature of the water which had turned extremely cold and was glad to get out of it. He gave the command for the dolphins and whale to return to base and walked the beach and up some steps, there were shops selling beach wear and beyond that, a cobbled road which led up a steep bank and headed towards a town.

Nathan climbed the bank and headed to the town. He was tired and found the hill draining. At long last, he made it to the town and finding a bank, drew out some Euro. He changed his clothes and bought a newspaper, 'Sangatte News' Nathan stared at the paper,' I'm in France!' he said to himself, 'the wale has travelled miles in a short space of time, I can't believe it.' He looked about him, on a notice board just above his head was map of how to get to the channel tunnel. Nathan made his way to the station which would take him home. He sat on the train watching the scenery fly by. He finally felt relaxed and even managed to get something to eat and drink he closed his eyes and thought how close he was to seeing Jemma again and knowing she was safe and sound. He yawned and sighed then his eyes opened wide and he sat forward quickly in his seat. Jemma was home sick and missing mam and dad, 'would she go back? Or would she go home!'. If he went home and she went back, she would be by herself and if he went back and she went home, they may split them up and he wouldn't be able to look after her. He looked out of the window as Dover drew near, 'what should he do.' The train finally pulled in to the station and Nathan looked for the nearest airport to Tee's side. Wilmington, Delaware, he read, he left the station and hired a taxi and soon he was in the airport waiting for his plane. He looked round at the people as they passed by, but there was only one thing on his mind, 'What should he do!'.

Barbara Goodall, had been back on the phone to Chris Carter. There had been no word from the five since the boys had disappeared. He had to admire the way they had done it, drawing the attention away from the signal button so they could get the signal out to the dolphins. The way they had escaped the yacht without being noticed, and how they had muffled their commands so he couldn't properly hear what they were saying. 'Yes' in a way, they had done well. None-the-less, they had completely disappeared. "There is no sign of them" he told Barbara Goodall. "What do you want me to do?". Barbara Goodall, thought for a few minutes, what could they do. "Come home" she told him," there is nothing you can do there". She went back to the animal sanctuary and waited with professor Collins.

A few hours had gone by and still no sign of the five or the dolphins. Barbara Goodall, was not happy. She paced the floor and constantly checked the signal which the sanctuary was sending out. She sat down, sick of standing and pacing and looked across at the dolphin arena. Suddenly, there was a bleep as the signal flashed on and off. "They are coming home" professor Collins yelled," They are coming home". Barbara Goodall jumped to her feet as the water in the arena began to create waves, and in a short time, the head of a dolphin appeared, followed by the second, then the whale. Barbara Goodall sighed with relief as the dolphins and whale, were given fish as a treat and a welcome home pat. She looked at professor Collins and nodded, there was only one problem left, 'where were the five, and would they come back?'.

Nathan finally got on his plane to Tee's side. He sat in his seat still not knowing what to do and stared out the window. A smile crossed his face when he thought of what they had done, who would believe they had ridden dolphins, sat on a Whale and worked with the most efficient security system the country had, and it was all done with animals. Jemma was also well on her way home, she thought of Nathan and wondered if he was safe, she couldn't believe what she had done, 'Her,' who would crawl out of anywhere to get where she wanted to be, but now, she had retrieved a vital document, escaped a spy, and had rode a dolphin. Ashley, was almost home, he wondered what Liam was doing and where he would go. He sucked on his straw as he drank his coke and felt his pocket to make sure the document was still there. He slightly shook his head as he thought about what he had, who would believe, that in his pocket was a document that would help a nation and He, had got it home. Naz too, had made it back and was on her last bit of journey. She wondered how the others were and hoped they had got home safely. She thought about dad, how proud he would be of her, if he knew what she had done. She could just imagine it. 'Hi dad, sorry I can't see you today, I have to find a spy, retrieve a document and work with dolphins', he would never believe it. Liam, like the others, was on his way, he had travelled some distance just to get the right plane home, but he had finally done it. He was tired and sick, he just wanted to get in his bed and he was worried over Ashley.

He sucked on a sweet and thought about the day, 'what a day', did he really do all the things he had done! He had trained with animals many people wouldn't even go to the country to see, walked Hand in hand with chimps, and had rode on a dolphin and whale, even he couldn't believe it. He sat back in his seat, it was amazing.

Chris Carters yacht had finally moored and he was now back at Hillock. Barbara Goodall, nodded as he approached. "The dolphins are back, we can only assume the five are ok and will make their way to Tee's side, you need to be there". Carter nodded back and left for Tee's side airport. Two planes had just landed, Carter watched the people as they approached customs, but no sign of the five. He went back to the car and waited, 'they are not coming' he thought to himself. A couple of hours later, another plane landed. Carter went back into the airport and looked on the landing board, 'London to Tees side. He frowned, 'surely they wouldn't come from there.' He haggled at the entrance before going back to the car when a face he recognised came towards him. Chris Carter smiled broadly, "Hallow Naz" he said; "I'm so pleased to see you, come on, the cars outside". Naz Weza walked to the car, but the other four, were not there. 'Damn!' she thought, I knew I should have gone home. She sat in the back of the car, she was miserable, she would be all alone, and even worse, was that she could be sent back to Chippingham. She slumped in her seat, tears forming in her eyes, how she wished she had gone home.

Chris Carter and Naz, sat in the car. There wasn't a flight due, but all they could do was wait. Naz was very tired, she just wanted to get comfy. She looked out the window of the car, tears forming every now and then as she watched people come and go. "Can I get out and stretch my legs?" she asked Carter. He nodded, it couldn't do any harm. Naz got out of the car and turned her back on Carter as she wiped more tears from her eyes. A taxi pulled up near her and she turned away hoping that no one could see she had been crying. "You made it back then" a voice behind her spoke, and on turning saw Ashley walking towards her. He looked at her, and gave her a hug, "where are the others, haven't they come back yet?" Naz shook her head as Ashley's face fell,' please don't say he went home' he thought to himself. "Welcome back Ashley" Chris Carter spoke, "hope the journey wasn't too strenuous". Ashley and Naz, sat in the car. It was getting late the two of them were exhausted. Ashley looked out of the window, 'where was Liam', he looked in the sky, lights were flashing and it looked like a plane was coming in. Carter got out of the car and went to the arrival board. Gatwick to Tees-side. He went back to the car, it's a local flight he announced. Ashley looked down hearted, as he watched the passengers unload, then smiling jumped out of the car and ran to the entrance. Liam sighed with relief and smiled back, "You did come back then" they both said at the same time, giving each other a gentle punch in the arm and walked towards the car. Just as they reached it, a taxi pulled up, the door opened and Jemma got out. The boys hugged her and hugged Naz too as she raced out to meet them. Jemma looked round," Where is Nathan?" she asked; they shook their heads as Jemma's heart sank, 'he must have gone home' she thought, what will she do! Tears filled her eyes, she couldn't do this alone. The four, stood looking at each other wondering what would happen next, when more lights in the sky appeared and another plane was about to land. The small group waited for what seemed a life time, when finally, people started to come out of the airport. Jemma's eyes were fixed on the door, but no Nathan. Her eyes filled with tears again as most of the people left. Ashley looked at Liam, then smiling nudged Liam, as Nathan came out of the entrance. Jemma shouted his Name, and raced towards him, flinging her arms around his neck, "You came back" he laughed;" for you" she said; Nathan grinned," me for you too" he replied; "Me for you". They walked over to where Liam, Ashley and Naz stood all talking at the same time, all, just glad to see each other.

Chris Carter, spoke on the phone to Barbara Goodall, "They have all come back, they came back for each other". Barbara Goodall smiled to herself, "I knew we had found the right ones" she replied; "Bring them in Chris". Several hours later, the small group entered Hillock, "let them sleep for tonight, and we will talk to them tomorrow" Barbara Goodall said; "They are too tired now".

The next day, the group entered the lounge room, they had breakfast and waited to see Barbara Goodall, 'were they in for a telling off!' oh well, it was worth it. Barbara Goodall entered the room, her face looked stern and had a constant frown on it. "Have you got the document" she asked; Ashley handed it to her. She looked round at their faces, then her frown turned into a smile. "You did well" she spoke "Are you ready, -ready for another ADVENTURE!".

Printed in the United States
By Bookmasters